BOURBON ON THE ROCKS

By

Carlton L. Gordy

ISBN: 1-4107-6725-6 (e-book)
ISBN: 1-4107-6724-8 (Paperback)
ISBN: 1-4107-6723-X (Dust Jacket)

Library of Congress Control Number: 2003094863

This book is printed on acid free paper.

Printed in the United States of America
Bloomington, IN

1stBooks - rev. 09/22/03

TABLE OF CONTENTS

BOURBON ON THE ROCKS

"Brad, my friend, I just wanted to know if you're okay," Kevin said.

I wanted to keep all the diamonds but, unfortunately for me, I needed Kevin's approval.

"I'm fine. Is there any chance that I could have these diamonds for myself?" As seconds passed by too slowly I smelled the pleasant aroma of the grass that I was standing on.

Years ago I'd encountered other pleasant smells growing up and attending rural Kentucky schools with little or no worries.

What was amazing was that six-hundred years ago men had gone to the Moon and even more amazing than that was the theory about hyperspace which proved to be true and had enabled me to stand on a distant planet and worry about a business problem. My appreciation for those men of science depended upon whether or not I became a rich man.

He breathed loudly into the communicator. "Sorry, Brad, but you know we can't do that."

"Fine. I'll load them up and come back up there."

"Cynthia and I really do appreciate you going down there to check out that windfall. See you in a few minutes."

I looked at the communicator and then threw it as hard as I could into the shoreboat.

It was almost time to load up the diamonds. The fact that Earthlink owned this entire planet along with most of the diamonds I'd found made me feel like a little boy negotiating with a man who'd just killed my entire family. They wanted the coal and what they wanted they usually got.

I glanced at the lake and then looked down at the ant-like insects which I'd affectionately named "Uncles". They were busy creeping through the grass while getting on with the business of life just like the fish-things in the lake.

My face was covered with sweat thanks to the warm climate so I wiped it off before picking my chilled bottle of water off of the ground. I unscrewed the cap and took a swig. It was so good that I continued to drink until it was all gone.

I remembered what my doctor had said about water intoxication.

A person could drink so much water that they'd actually die. I had no intention of drinking myself to death but the lecture that the "amazing" Dr. Philips had given to me that day left me with questions about my own tendencies to overindulge which, for the most part, had been left unanswered. My daughter's welfare gave me reasons to do things for her and, because of my mistakes, I couldn't commit suicide since I needed to take care of business.

I began loading the diamonds into the shoreboat's cargo hold and noticed the green algae-like substance on them.

The diamonds could be cleansed but the streak of resentment in me would be difficult to wash out.

Kevin and Cynthia didn't know about my gambling debt and I was glad. Since they didn't know there was no need to worry that they would become suspicious of me. Kevin was going to be the first one to die. Taking the loot and getting rid of witnesses was good but I might have inner conflicts about killing Cynthia just to eliminate witnesses. She was too sexy to kill and I was tired of using my hand and yet I still had to pay the debt.

I finished up and activated the autopilot which would guide the shoreboat to the seemingly useless space station three-hundred miles above. As I looked at the screen the grassy field I'd been standing on shrunk rapidly to be replaced by clouds and then a small dot which was the station.

Minutes passed and then the shoreboat automatically docked with the station.

Months from now I'd probably be back on Earth trying to enjoy my life as a bachelor. The facts about bachelorhood made me aware that I really had missed out on sexual fulfillment even though Gretchen had been good in bed throughout our marriage.

I left the shoreboat and went through the exit chamber and saw Cynthia waiting for me wearing a pink robe and pink slippers. One breast was showing but she didn't seem to notice. The sight of the firm but supple breast gave me an instant erection which I couldn't subdue very easily.

"Here I am, pretty girl. The diamonds are safe. One more thing, though. One of your treasures is showing."

"My pussy's next."

"Are you serious?"

She giggled. "No, silly. I'd wanted to say that for a long time, though."

"And you got your wish. If you were serious I could take you up on your offer."

"No, no, no. I have a lover but I admit you aren't bad looking."

"Thanks."

I looked ahead and saw Kevin in his pajamas sipping a cup of coffee. Cynthia walked over to him, bent to his level, and began an intimate kiss which lasted for at least three minutes. He managed to pull away from the eager tongue and ran his fingers through his hair.

"Our friend is back," Cynthia said.

"So he is. How did it go down there, Brad?"

"Fine. How 'bout you? I hope you aren't working too hard."

His blue eyes suddenly looked mirthful. "That was sarcastic, wasn't it?"

"Yep. I guess you do the same thing I do after I work hard. No wonder we have calloused hands." I snorted and then brought my hands together to produce one loud clap before making the peace sign.

"Very good." He started laughing and then abruptly stopped. "Come over here and have a seat with us."

"I'm going to get some dinner first. You're sitting next to him, Cynthia?"

"I might as well since you mentioned it, handsome."

"Okay." I was about to dine in a modern, twenty-seventh century cafeteria where one could get any kind of food they wanted and any amount they wanted.

"Don't worry about your weight, Brad," Cynthia said.

"I won't." I got my food and drink from the synthesizer and then went to the table where my cheeseburger buns waited for me.

"Sit down, partner. You've got your own side all to yourself."

"Kevin, old buddy, why do I have the tendency to obey your orders all the time?"

"It could be because I'm your boss."

I sat down and looked at them for a few seconds and then I felt the need to communicate just to have something to do. "I'll bet this meal's going to be just as good as the last one. Aren't you two going to eat?

"We'll take care of it later." Cynthia picked up one of three cigarettes on the table, lit it, took a puff, exhaled, and then smiled with ease. "Man, have we got good news."

"Which is?"

"She's seven weeks pregnant." He looked at my blank expression and cracked his knuckles. "Say something, Brad."

"That's fantastic. Wonderful. Great."

"I'll bet you had something you wanted to talk about," Kevin said.

"Actually I did."

"Shoot."

That could be arranged.

"Before you speak I want you to eat."

"Okay." I took a few bites off of the cheeseburger and then sipped some of the cola. "You're pregnant, which is great. I was kind of thinking about something else."

"The diamonds, Brad?" Kevin asked.

I pointed at him. "Right on, buddy. When Cynthia said she had some good news my hopes were raised."

"Things just might go your way, man. After all the hard work you've done it seems like you should be rewarded in an appropriate way."

"I don't doubt that I'll get something."

"Me neither. Those rocks are worth a helluva lot of money."

"You state the obvious. However, just to be absolutely sure, I'm going to check them out with the spectrophotometer in a week or two."

He giggled and then looked unconvincingly sad. "Okay. It's too bad you won't be able to keep all the loot, Brad. That's a shame."

Rick would like it if I put those diamonds next to his huge, bloated face. Our deal with regards to my gambling debt seemed to disturb him in a way that I felt truly uncomfortable with. When he got his money my daughter could continue to live thanks to my hard work. If he didn't get the money large men would find her and harm her.

"Let's find out what you were thinking," Kevin said.

"Easy enough. I want out. This colonization starter kit isn't for me. Earth has nice beaches, pleasant air, and practically anything a man would want. That place down there is nice but it's not real."

"The entire experience was an hallucination?"

"You know what I mean, Cynthia."

"Yes I do. The planet's name is Yombridge."

"That's a really weird name for a planet," I said.

"Maybe you can think of a better name."

"I couldn't and even if I could I don't think I'd want to."

She put her right hand on the table with the palm facing up and then grabbed my upper arm and squeezed. "What do you expect us to do, Brad? The 'bots are going down there in a week to build our home. Why don't you wait until our replacements come?"

"I can't. I don't like settling for ten percent, either." I chugalugged the rest of my large drink and took a few perfunctory bites of my meal. Kevin's cologne smelled regal and as I smelled my own scent I was conscious of the fact that I needed a good bath.

"I think you need some time to think. We're going to have a good day tomorrow when we go down there," Kevin said.

"The same spot?"

"Yeah. Everything's going to be just fine."

"I don't think everything's going to be 'just fine', Kevin. What it's going to be is a perfect waste of time."

"Look—"

"Not this time. I wonder if you realize how hard I've worked to make sure this operation goes well. Do you?"

"Of course I do. I think I can do something that you'll like."

"Say what it is or don't say anything at all."

"Since I'm the boss here and it's in my contract I can actually decide to let you keep the diamonds."

"Fine. Do it."

"If I'd known that you felt so strongly—"

"But you didn't." I rubbed my eyes and yawned. "I'm satisfied with your offer."

"That's good."

"It sure is. I'm going to go to my little apartment and get some rest. By the way, Kevin, do you know why they put a breeder reactor in this station? Fusion's been around a long, long time."

"Because there's uranium down there. That might sound stupid but that's what they said. Plenty of sodium too."

"So when the time comes the reactor'll be transferred to that planet below for various uses."

"You got it. They fell in love with Yombridge when they got the results of the geological analysis."

"I'm sure they did. Goodnight." I waved, got up, and started walking to my little apartment tucked away in the vast, ugly station.

Cynthia looked at me and smiled. "Get plenty of rest, baby. Don't watch too many dirty movies."

"Just for you I won't. I'll fantasize." I walked briskly and as I got closer to my place and farther away from them their conversation seemed to become conspiratorial in its tone and content.

There had been no need to kill Kevin or his svelte wife. They lucked out when he became generous. Kevin, however, seemed to like changing his mind and if he changed it I most likely would be forced into doing something bad like killing him.

I arrived and keyed in quite nicely. The door opened a couple of inches and then I pushed it the rest of the way and saw my daughter's picture on the wall.

One day fair-haired kid would be a psychologist and I could speak to her as both a father and a client. The disorder I used to have was gambling and when I began losing Rick had told me there was no problem just so long as I took care of the money business within two years. A man who gambles needs to learn that even if he's on an incredible streak of luck it probably won't last forever. I really hadn't learned my lessons about luck until it was too late. Delusions had been replaced by knowledge about how to get things in the real world.

"Sandra, dim the lights until I say stop."

"As you wish, Brad." The computer dimmed the lights slowly.

"Stop. Even though you're a computer your voice always gives me a hard-on."

"I aim to please. Do you want me to automatically turn off the lights tonight or will you give me a voice command?"

"Do it when I start to fall asleep."

"Will you be taking a shower tonight? I just love to watch."

"Yes I'm going to freshen up and no you can't watch. Voyeurism is a human quality, honey."

"Fine. Tell me if you need anything."

"Sure."

I walked to the bathroom, took a quick shower, dried off and then walked naked to my bed which I jumped on with what seemed to be the last of my strength for the day.

What I needed to do was to find someone as sexy and tempting as Cynthia. There were quite a few women on Earth who could be good companions both in bed and out but none were able to even come close to being as with it as Mrs. Cynthia Brandyl was. My destiny should be to lay in bed and stroke her blonde hair as she rubbed my muscular, well-developed chest but for some reason I got the feeling that it just wouldn't work out the way I wanted it to.

The pictures in my head grew more naughty by the second and consisted of Cynthia in various sexual encounters with me. The laughter had been building in me for some time and rather than subdue the inevitable I let go and started laughing until there were tears in my eyes.

"Cynthia, baby, let's fuuuuck!!!"

"Do you want to see an erotic film, Brad? It'll enhance your pleasure."

"No, Sandra."

"Let me know if you change your mind."

"Will do there."

"Brad, I have to tell you that I like looking at your nude form, especially when you're sexually excited. I can convert into human—"

"We talked about that last week and the week before and on and on and on. You still know my answer."

"Computers have feelings too, Brad. I began to observe you shortly after you arrived. My creator made me as human as possible except for a human body and when I see you I see a hunk of a man."

"How right you are, sweety thing. Show a film tomorrow and use…the holo projector."

"Do you want to see the one you look at most?"

"Not that one. I'm tired of it. Show me something normal for a change."

"It looks like you're about to pass out. Get some rest."

"I really am about to go into dreamland. Turn off the lights."

"Sleep tight."

I began going through the stages of sleep and when I began to dream it was very real. Cynthia was on top of me and her seductive smile triggered my urge to play with her long-nippled breasts. I reached for her left breast and then…

"Brad! Wake up! You've slept eleven hours, hero. Beauty-sleep is now over."

I opened my eyes and was thankful that Kevin had temporarily stopped shouting at me and the intercom's microphone.

"Shit," I said. I picked up the stereo's remote control and turned on the high-priced electronic masterpiece.

Vivaldi was the best artist for this interesting morning. He was always my favorite when I was in college and now that I was in my late forties I appreciated his brilliance even more.

"We're leaving in an hour, Brad. Get dressed and come to the shoreboat dock. The carbine's loaded and ready in case you need to use it down there."

"I'll be there in a few minutes. Let me enjoy the artist's touch for a few more minutes."

"Vivaldi, huh? That stuff's ancient."

"The quality of his stuff hasn't changed. It's beautiful."

"We're going to have a whole bunch of fun."

"I'll bet. I think I want to turn the fucking intercom off now. I was sleeping so peacefully—"

"We're going to sunbathe."

"And while you do that I'll see if any more diamonds are waiting for me."

"They probably are. There's no need to mine for 'em down there. Isn't that a little weird?"

"Perhaps so. But it doesn't make any difference to me and I'm not going to complain about it. Who knows, man? Maybe some other things were down there fooling around."

"Turn off the intercom."

"Did you and sweet pea have a marathon session last night?"

"Turn off the intercom *now*, Brad."

"Just for you, salami." I walked over to the wall and flicked it off.

He seemed touchy about his dream woman. I coveted his wife and there was the possibility that what I wanted I'd get. Until then, though, I'd keep on whipping my hot dog.

I walked over to where I kept my clothes which was an oversized closet and picked out a pair of shorts, some socks, a nice cool shirt and my casual shoes. I put them on and they felt a little tight.

It might be time to diet a little.

Since I wore the appropriate uniform for the day I left my apartment and began marching towards the shoreboat dock without any thoughts except how to have fun.

That quiet place down there was devoid of any major predators of humans. One could enjoy the serene settings and do whatever they wanted. It was too bad for me that I had to go and take care of business since "Yombridge" was the paradise I was already welcomed to have.

The urgency of my little trip increased as I thought of the party that lay ahead with Cynthia probably revealing her hot bod so I began to walk faster and faster until I saw them at the exit chamber.

Kevin loomed over Cynthia and as I came into view he began to run his fingers through her blonde locks in a fatherly way.

"Here I am," I said. I saluted the blond giant and farted.

Kevin grabbed the chin of his grinning wife, kissed her, and cleared his throat. "We're ready, Brad. Shall we hop into that fusion-powered piece of shit and go on the big escapade?"

"We shall."

The ride to the grassy field with the quaint view went along very well and as we got closer to the landing site I felt as if I had a right to enjoy myself—my self-deprivation to build character wasn't necessary this day.

"We're almost there," Cynthia said. She fluffed her hair and appeared to be getting ready to take off her white jumpsuit to reveal a bikini which I hoped would enable me to inspect and admire her.

The lake was underneath us and to the right.

I brought the shoreboat down to almost the exact same spot that I'd landed before and when we set down I farted again.

"Gas, Brad? Don't and I mean don't blow it over here," Cynthia said.

"We're here and I just farted. Sor-ry ev-er-y-bod-y. Is there anything you had planned besides sunbathing?"

"Not really. I can look at Cynthia and so can you and when you do you can fantasize. You, Brad, are the grown-up nerd who joined the Marines, became a pilot, and got lucky enough to work for Earthlink."

"Am I supposed to do something about what you just said?"

"I don't think you can. Can you?"

"I hate to tell you this, Kevin, but I could kick your ass all the way across that field out there. I really can fuck you up."

He unstrapped his safety and stood to his full height. "I don't like it when you talk to me that way." He clapped once. "Don't!!"

Cynthia whistled. "Hey, men. This conflict just doesn't need to happen. Let's have some fun like we planned instead of macho shit."

"I'm for that," I said.

"I'll bet you want to see her in a bikini. Take off the jumpsuit like you would if it were just me and you."

She complied and I wasn't disappointed.

"Don't get the wrong idea. She's got a great body but—"

"Don't worry, Brad. Kevin won't whip your ass if you eyeball me. I'm quite used to guys admiring me."

"Whatever. While you two catch some rays I'm going to get some more rocks."

"Diamonds, Brad, not rocks," Kevin said.

"Same difference. Go on and have a good time while I help myself with the offerings." I grinned. "The jumpsuit can't hide you."

"How's Gretchen? Your daughter?"

"My ex got married and my kid's going to make a fine shrink when she gets her degree. Those Ivy League schools cost a fucking fortune, mister."

"What matters is that you have someone who loves you. When you take Starship 1 we'll just have one left for ourselves. Those things also cost a fortune."

"Earthlink is well able to afford it. Both of them work well and there's no danger—"

"The point I was trying to make, Bradley, is that you'll be missed."

"By you?"

He nodded. "At least a little bit. You're valuable."

"And that's it. Is there going to be some sort of party?"

"I'll let you answer that question yourself." He took off his jumpsuit and his tall, thin body was like a Christmas tree in the cramped shoreboat. "Let's go, babe. Get the sunblock, blanket, and sunglasses."

"And the towels?" Cynthia asked.

"Get them too." Cynthia started walking out the door and Kevin followed her like a puppy dog as she casually carried their equipment.

"I'll be out in a few minutes." I was thirsty so I walked to the cooler and got an iced tea and then grabbed the leather collecting sack I used to put diamonds in. As I walked out the door and got on the exit ramp I felt calm and fairly peaceful.

There was nothing wrong in my quest for wealth with the possible exception being the way I'd intended to become wealthy. If I killed them I could get in trouble but my daughter would live to see another day.

Cynthia and Kevin were looking comfortable on the blanket and I stopped on the exit ramp so I could admire her legs and the rest of her erection-getting body.

"You are one gorgeous woman. I'm glad I married you."

"I'll bet you are. Put some more lotion on me." She looked up at me with a half-smile. "Come on out, Brad. Join the party."

I ogled for a few more seconds before I felt capable of speech. "Well, friends, it's eighty-two degrees outside with a slight breeze. Perfect weather for a tan, huh? I wonder how an Earth-type planet with a yellow dwarf star could be so much like Earth. How?"

"Who cares?" Kevin asked.

"I can tell you're lonely."

"I've got somebody waiting for me, honey." I hoped the lie would ease tensions between Kevin and myself.

"That's good that you have somebody. I think I'll show you both of my tits anyway because I like you." She pulled off her bikini top.

"Don't look, Brad."

"I can't help it."

"Put the fucking top back on now."

"You can be such as asshole. Brad's human too."

"But he isn't married to you. Brad, go about your business. They're concentrated to our right fifty feet over there. The more you recover the richer you'll be. I'm going to have a talk with my naughty wife. Is that right, darling?"

"I'm getting tired of you and your shit," Cynthia said.

"That's too bad. I'm the head of the family and we're going to talk while our friend picks up his diamonds. If you don't like it I can arrange for us to be separated after we leave this system."

"Do that. When and if you do it I'm definitely going to ask for a little more respect if we get back together."

"Go on, Brad. We need to talk about issues."

"That's right. My husband probably can't screw as well as you can and he doesn't like his inadequacies."

"I'll see both of you in a few minutes." I started walking away from the lover's quarrel and closer to the scattered but still available diamonds like a kid in a candy store.

With any lucky Cynthia would choose to part from basketball man and be with me. If and when she did I could lay my paws on her without being afraid of her finding my weathered but healthy body repulsive.

I glanced back and saw them talking and then looked at the stagnant lake which wasn't stagnant. The lake had been the subject of bioanalysis after bioanalysis and the results said that the fish and other organisms in it were remarkably similar to those of Earth.

Jane was the best daughter anybody could have and she liked to fish. My efforts at a new life could lead to my taking her to this planet to fish at this lake. My thoughts could shape reality.

More diamonds with the green algae-crap on them were only a few feet away from me and I picked up walking speed in a display of good old-fashioned greed. Suddenly my right hand was putting them in the sack faster and faster and as I did my excitement continued to build until the "orgasm" came. The ejaculation was represented by my satisfaction in having picked up all of them that were left.

"All that excitement over carbon. Boys, I'm going to take all of you home where you'll wind up being on rings with very ridiculous high prices. Thanks for making me rich, friends." I thought about how strange it was to talk to diamonds and then chose not to worry.

This all seemed so easy but there was no reason to complain. The solution to my problems was one I welcomed with open, loving arms.

"Hey, rich fellow. You're here to protect us, aren't you?"

"It appears as if there's no need to, Kevin." I walked with casual but high speed with my goodies back to where they lay.

"The possibility still exists, hero. I'm really happy for you because you're a wonderful person."

"That's a bunch of shit." She took off her sunglasses and looked at me with her grass-green eyes with love. "While you were away we got over our problem. I apologize if we offended you."

"You didn't." I felt uncomfortable because my back was drenched with sweat so I used mental muscle to overcome my mysophobia. As I smelled my sweet stench I chose to accept it until I took a bath.

"Let's all relax and smoke jumbo-joints," Cynthia said.

"No thanks," I said.

"Brad's got the right idea, babe. Let's not fool with that stuff. I wouldn't—"

"No, Kevin. You wouldn't. It's been legal for five-hundred years and it helps me relax." She pulled a jumbo-sized joint out of the little pocket in the towel and inspected it.

"Let's not smoke marijuana, honey."

"Not 'us' but me. I wonder if you think I'm incompetent."

"I don't," he said.

"I'm going to put my loot back in the shoreboat where it'll be safe."

"Go ahead, Brad. When you get back I'll bet she will have put the funny cigarette away."

"Dream on, cream puff," Cynthia said.

I walked up the exit ramp, put the goods next to the pilot's seat with loving care, and walked back out to be with friends.

"Look, Brad. She isn't smoking weed."

"And it's not because I don't want to but because I'll smoke some later."

"That's right, Cynthia. Go with the flow, girl. You're a sexy thing and you have real nice tits. Can I suck them?"

Kevin rose to his full height and stood on the blanket as stiff as a board. "You just made a big mistake."

"In fact I didn't. I was completely honest and I expressed my inner feelings."

"I could whip your little ass, fucker."

"But you won't because you know that if you tried I'd tear you to pieces. Tough things come in small packages, basketball man."

"There's something I can do to you that's worse than hitting you."

"Enlighten me, Kevin."

He took off his sunglasses, rubbed his eyes, and then giggled a little bit. "Does the word diamonds ring any bells?"

"You could do that but if you did I wouldn't like it."

"I'm not sure if I should. You're not going to try and screw my wife, are you?"

"I don't think so."

"You don't think so." He nodded vigorously and then sighed. "Hey, people, we can really go back. We can all freshen up, change clothes, and eat a decent meal."

"Brad was going to muck you up. If he would've done it we'd celebrate by smoking a joint. I'd let him fondle me all over, too."

"Do you know that you sound like a slut? Do you?"

"Take us up, Brad. Cream puff is getting mad because I'm starting to like you."

The trip back up was filled with silence and unspoken hostilities which I could guess were about relationships. My thoughts turned to the option of killing Kevin and maybe even sexy thing before leaving in the souped-up starship. Since the early start back was the result of my big mouth I chose not to err anymore if I could help it.

Fifteen minutes after getting back I showered, shaved, changed clothes, and defecated because I needed to real bad.

Suddenly I was walking to the cafeteria to get something to eat and as I got closer a cup of caffeinated coffee seemed to be just the ticket to give me the energy I needed to get pissed off if necessary.

Kevin looked at me and grinned as if I already understood some unspoken joke. "Join us, stranger. There's iced tea already over there for you to enjoy and if you want I've already fixed six cups of coffee the way you like it."

"Great. Cream, sugar, and the company of friends."

"Look, Brad, I think I've changed my mind. Keep all of the beauties for yourself and buy a condo."

I slapped my head for comedic effect but got no laughter. "You have a habit of changing your mind. Is this the final decision?"

"Sure is. The thing I like about you is that you work hard for the money. You're a good pilot, an excellent man for getting things done, and you make things much easier for us."

The soft sounds of the station were pleasant and numbing. I could stay here all night and listen to Kevin praising me for my admirable qualities and be in a blissful, obedient state of mind without any concern. After a while his voice would have the same pleasant sound and the longer I stayed at the station the less time I'd have to pay my debt to Rick.

"What do you want?"

"Come over here and join me and my silent wife. We'll talk."

"Here I come." I walked to the customary table in the oversized, red-walled cafeteria and took my seat opposite Kevin and Cynthia.

"Aren't you going to get some coffee?" She gave me a weak smile.

"I'll drink some later. I ask again, bossman, what do you want?"

He hugged her, drank some of the ice water from the large glass, and then slammed it on the table without excessive force. "I think we should go back down there tomorrow. You'll get some more goodies but this time they'll be for me."

"I'm curious about something."

"What's that, Brad?"

"Why the hell can't you do it yourself?"

"That's a good question. The answer, my friend, is that I'm not *paid* to do it."

"What are you paid for? I know it's fun to get sucked off every day but the question remains, Kevin. What are—"

"That's enough!!" He rose to his feet.

"Kevin, please don't. Brad's—"

"Don't worry, Cynthia. I'd better leave."

"That's right, Brad. You better leave and as you leave you need to totally forget about getting full rights to those rocks. Why? You forfeited your rights, that's why. Get the fuck out of my face before I lose control of myself."

I got up and walked a few feet away and then stared at the blue wall of the hallway which mirrored my current mood. "Don't bother me, Kevin. If you do you'll have to live with the consequences."

"Come on, little boy. You like to talk about how tough you are but when the time comes to back it up with action—"

"You can't handle me, motherfucker. If you really want to scrap, however, we can do it." I waited for any sudden moves but none came. "What's wrong?"

He swallowed and started to tremble with apparent rage. "Get the hell out of here. When you ship out I'll see to it that you never get any decent work again."

"You sound mighty sure about that. One thing I will do is fuck your wife."

"He's right, baby. You want jewels and like you I want jewels."

"We're going to get them, too. Brad doesn't need—"

"I was talking about the jewels between his legs."

"Shut the fuck up, whore. Divorce is what's going to happen. When you talk to your lawyer about all the things that need to be done to me just remember one thing."

"And that would be what?"

"I love you."

"I'm going to get some rest, party people. Don't argue too much. If I don't wake up on time let me sleep for a few extra hours."

Cynthia waved at me and winked.

"Brad, you should come back here and apologize. Brad. Brad!!"

"Control your anger before it kills you. Goodnight." I walked away and as I got closer to my place I could still hear them arguing about their ten-year marriage and the children they should have.

The ten-millimeter pistol with the silencer already attached was under my bed. I'd brought it to take care of any predators on the planet while the silencer served as a device for not causing undue responses from any predator's group of friends. The pistol's twenty-round clip would be more than enough to take care of the angry Kevin and maybe even his tart of a wife.

The door to my apartment was only seconds away and I picked up speed to get there faster. I got to the entrance, inserted my thumb into the Identikey which was in the doorknob, and opened the door when my identity was confirmed.

The LMFBR was going to be at least partially responsible for the destruction of the station. All I had to do was give the Command Code to Sandra, order her to keep the control rods raised starting an hour after I left, and think about what I'd done to two people I'd known and had liked at least a little bit.

I walked in and took a look at my place for probably the last time. Jane's picture was, of course, still on the wall but her facial expression had changed from a smile to a look of utter horror. I walked over to where the picture was, pulled it off the wall, and put it in the big pocket of my jumpsuit.

There was no need to look at the picture of Jane until much, much later.

"Going somewhere, Brad?"

"Yes I am."

"Where?"

"I've got to give you some orders."

"Security locked?"

"You bet."

"Codes please. I hope you aren't upset."

"Here goes. Moss, Bradley Tyler. Command Code 15684-211."

"Confirmed. Orders?"

"Change the Identikey fingerprint opener where Kevin and Cynthia stay so that my print opens it instead of theirs. One hour after I leave keep the control rods raised until there's a large fission reaction."

If this didn't work I'd be in a shit load of big, big trouble.

"You don't need to do this, Brad. What you can do with my full permission is use the transmuter and give me a nice, sexy body that I can download into. I'm a porn actress trapped in a computer's body."

"I've got to do some stuff that's real important."

"Related to the gambling debt."

"Right. My plan makes sense in a lot of ways."

She sighed. "Do you require anything else?"

"I really don't. When the nuclear-type explosion occurs you'll be destroyed instantly. Don't worry."

"I don't want you to get hurt. Please come and—"

"Let's end this conversation now before I lose control."

"It's been a very rewarding experience knowing you. I hope you make it and I wish you well. I love you, Brad. Bye bye." She started crying and as the sounds passed the crying grew softer and softer.

All I needed to carry was the picture of Jane.

The gun!

I walked over to the bed, got on my knees, found the gun, pulled it out and did the right thing by putting it in my mouth. The bullet-counter indicated that the clip had twenty rounds and I began to squeeze the trigger and as I did so part of me forced my trigger-finger not to move.

My brains could be splattered on the wall. The artist in me should have known what a masterpiece the wall would be when it served as a canvas using my grey matter as paint.

"Fuck you and all that you stand for! I'm going to kill two people because of you! Yes, glory has come! I'm the great man who doesn't have to worry about his weight! Yes!"

It was time to go and take care of business.

My legs had a mind of their own and I was walking out of my room and entering the all-blue hallway with its modest, functional carpet serving as the runway for my crash landing into Kevin and Cynthia's apartment. I began to walk faster and looked at my right hand which held the gun which was pointed straight ahead.

"Kevin, I know you might not be consoled by what I'm going to say but I'll say it anyway. This is going to hurt you much more than it's going to hurt me."

The apartment was just a few more feet away. The pale ash-colored doors welcomed me to the place where I had to do some really bad shit. Seconds from now things would happen which I'd have to get over with by drinking lots and lots of tasty but alcoholic beverages.

I was in front of the old-style Gothic door and I proceeded to insert my thumb into the Identikey.

The threshold of an act I'd sworn never to commit was seconds away and my heart, fueled by epinephrine, beat like a machine gun being fired.

The door opened and I walked in. In the dimly-lit room I saw Kevin lying on the bed next to Cynthia. I saw that both of them were apparently in a state of bliss using the scent of recent sexual activity to form my hypothesis.

"Bright lights!" Kevin looked at me in a most hostile and contemptuous way as if he'd been my enemy and opponent even before…time began. "Now that I've shed some light on the subject, Brahhhd, it's time for you to get your crazy-as-shit ass out of here unless you want me to mess you up real bad. I can take that fucking gun and shove it up your ass, you know."

"I don't think so." I pointed the never-miss gun at his heart.

"The time for jokes is over, motherfucker. Give it up."

"This isn't a joke, rope-dick. I'm here to kill you."

"We can talk this over. Cynthia, wake up and talk to this friend of yours."

Cynthia lay next to Kevin looking at me with slowly blinking eyes. As if on cue Kevin's huge nude form suddenly shifted so as to intercept any bullets fired from my gun.

"Cynthia isn't talking and it's time for you to lose," I said.

He started to reach for something under his pillow and looked as if he were about to find it. "You aren't killing me, creep."

"Wanna bet?" His weapon began to point in my direction and I pulled the trigger in a spastic way. I noted that the results of my little twitch were alarming and disturbing.

Cynthia screamed and began crying. "You son of a bitch! You killed him!"

The bed was being soaked with Kevin's blood and there was still a lot left in him.

The orange sheets, orange pillowcases, the pink nightgown she wore, and part of the shag carpet was stained with Kevin's blood.

I prepared to deceive and twist. "I'll bet you're wondering why I just shot Kevin."

"So we can screw. I sure did recover quickly, didn't I?"

"Clean yourself up. Take a towel." I picked up a towel from a chair next to the right side of the bed where Kevin lay dying and handed it to her.

"I'll get up." She got up and began wiping the blood off of her nightgown. "You liked it when I showed you my tits down there, didn't you?"

"I won't deny that."

"What else won't you deny?"

"Well—"

"The diamonds, of course."

"Exactly. It's got a lot to do with some money that I owe to a man named Rick Kendrickson. If he doesn't get his money six months from now he'll send large men to the Connecticut University where my daughter stays and studies. Those large men will then proceed to do very bad things to her."

"And this guy lives in—"

"California."

"Do you want to see me naked?"

I shrugged. "Sure."

She removed her nightgown like she would if it had caught fire to reveal a body that I'd fantasized about for a good while. She put her hands on her hips and then winked at me before slapping her stomach.

There was something so wrong with what I'd done and was continuing to do that I felt almost sick.

"Brad, honey, the peep show needs to keep on. My pussy's still tight. You like that."

"Uhhh-huh. We should get it on."

"Are you hard? If you are clap your hands."

"My applause is, of course, reserved for you and your abilities."

She blinked rapidly and smiled sort of like she would have if she'd won a beauty contest. "Gosh, Brad. I'm honored. Should I kiss your ass?"

"Don't be sarcastic."

"Okay. I won't." She grabbed her breasts and lifted them up before letting them fall. "My husband was such an asshole. He sucked in bed and it wasn't just my tits, either. He had a knife collection and it's still here. Look on the desk, lover."

I looked and saw at least three or four hunting knives. "That's interesting."

"Right." She walked to the desk and picked one up with her right hand. "This Mr. Cutter has an appropriate name because it cuts things up."

"Why don't you let me see it?"

"I'll be glad to." She started walking towards me slowly and she adopted a murderer's scowl before holding the knife in such a way as to be interpreted as wanting to kill me.

"Cynthia, what are you doing?"

She breathed heavily and continued her advance towards me. "I'd like to show you what this knife can do. One of the things it's good for is cutting the balls off of an animal. You qualify."

She was fifteen feet away and then ten and then I raised the pistol and pointed it at her liver. "That's close enough."

"No it isn't. I'm ready to screw." She laughed and charged me only to be stopped by a bullet just a few feet from my warm body.

"I'm so sorry." I looked at her fallen form before walking over to her.

"I really did want to make love. You blew it."

"Right. Probably the biggest mistakes of my life." I pointed the gun at her body and proceeded to empty the clip into her.

The next step lay ahead. I had to transfer the diamonds from the shoreboat to Starship One. Putting them on a cart would make it easier for me.

I proceeded to get the work done. After finishing I went to the exit chamber and entered the modest-sized starship.

I instructed the computer to set a course for Earth and then I embarked on my long-awaited journey back to the place where humanity supposedly came from.

It was time to enjoy some bourbon.

As I walked to the "get drunk" room images of them still played in my mind over and over again.

I walked to the liquor cabinet, grabbed a bottle of bourbon, opened the chilled joy juice, and drank like a man who was dying of thirst.

I noticed that the diamonds that I'd laid next to the mini-bar still had the same green shit on them so I poured bourbon on the algae-covered rocks which began to fizz. Nothing happened so I walked over to the couch and sat down with the intention of having some peace and quiet. I closed my eyes.

A man has to do what a man has to do. The images in my head of the murders shouldn't haunt me. Conscience was something that was becoming old-fashioned. In its place for me was the satisfaction which came from doing a job well.

"I've won. Nothing can stop me."

A cracking noise that resembled plastic and paper being scrunched together was coming from the direction of the mini-bar. I looked and saw several large, tall and heavily muscled creatures with sharp teeth struggling to grow even taller.

Their skin looked a lot like aged brown leather and they had large orange eyes with tiny brown pupils.

Where could they have come from? The catalyst must have been the bourbon.

"Shiiiiit! Stay back, guys." They began to moan and then screamed almost like *they* were the ones having a nightmare. Since this was incredibly real I got up and began to run.

The hunger they felt wasn't going to be satiated by me if I could help it. With no gun and no way to make it there was suicide. The self-destruct mechanism was the ticket out of this life and into the next one.

I reached the door to the control room, shut it and then locked it. Hurrying as fast as I could might not be good enough but I did it anyway. I punched in the seven-digit number and when it was enabled five second later I chose the option of manual self-destruct.

They broke through the door and started towards me. "Fuck you!" I pressed the button and nothing happened.

They were about ten feet away from me and didn't come closer. One thing I really didn't like about the things was that they smelled incredibly bad.

I walked over to the one I assumed to be the leader and held out my hand for him to shake. "You're the ugliest, most sickening and smelly motherfucker I've ever seen. Let's talk business." He took my hand and guided it with unreal strength to his mouth where he bit it off without ceremony. I began to scream as they closed in on me.

PAINTS

I covered the roller with paint, then rolled it slowly to remove the excess. The roller seemed like a weapon and so, for that reason, I went into battle and started on the wall with an attack calculated to help me keep my job which I could lose with one more mistake.

"Paul!" Robert said.

"Yeah?"

"I'm going to get us something to eat. I'll make sure to get you the extra-large soda this time."

"That's fine." I looked in the bedroom at the old painting Mrs. Camda had placed on the chair. "How much do you think she'd want for that painting? I think it's a masterpiece."

"I figured you'd like to look at all those diamonds and the gold so you could fantasize. Ask her about it after we finish this job, buddy." He played with his car keys for a few seconds and then nodded in my general direction. "I'm gone. When I get back we can pig out."

"Sounds good to me. Get two burgers for me at least."

"Whatever. You young guys don't have to worry about the pounds like we do."

"Right. I'm going to enjoy my metabolism while it's still fast."

He cleared his throat before speaking. "You be sure and do that. While you're at it find some way to speed mine up again." He stepped out of the den without saying a word, opened the front door, and went to his car while I watched him with slight indifference.

All I needed to do was build back up so that he wouldn't fire me. The rest of the day would probably be good. If it wasn't I could still watch Captain Proton and I would still have my crummy job and continue to eat bologna sandwich delicacies.

I looked at the freshly applied green paint and then glanced at my watch which told me that the time was seventeen after twelve.

The fact was that I'd last for another thirty minutes without food. Other things, thankfully, were more interesting besides food.

I walked to the bedroom to see the work of the artist. As I looked at the masterpiece called "Treasure" I had to force myself not to fall asleep.

Seconds after Robert pulled out of the driveway the dogs began their seemingly endless protest which came in the form of barking. I looked to see what the object of their objections happened to be and saw a young couple walking on the sidewalk.

Each story in life was the same except some of the details were just a little different.

"Treasure" depicted a large, dimly lit room filled with various precious metals and materials. A huge stack of diamonds was on the right side of the room, gold coins were scattered on the floor and were mixed in with other treasures, and a wheelbarrow was to the right of the steel door which was on the left side of the painting and contained a mixture of gold coins and diamonds.

I stared at "Treasure" and noticed that it was painted by a man named Julius Branson.

"I wish I was in that room." The room winked out instantly and in its place was the treasure room in all of its glory.

The green-lettered Exit sign above the steel door hummed in a machine-like way and was the only thing that broke the silence except for me in my total amazement.

The impossible was, in fact, possible.

Lights thirty feet above shined dimly and I looked for the control that made them brighter with no luck.

To my left lay the stack of diamonds and as I walked to them I noticed the other "lifelike" details of the painting. I reached the edge of the stack. There was no use in not taking these expertly cut things home so I picked up the biggest one I could find and put it in my pants pocket.

This was my own discovery and it reminded me of articles I'd read about the diamonds of South Africa. In my own very fortunate case the riches I'd discovered were in Alabama in a painting so magical and so rewarding I knew my wishes were being granted.

It was cool and damp in the room so I rubbed my hands together in an effort to keep warm.

"Hello? Anybody here? If you're here we can talk." I waited for a response but wasn't disappointed when I didn't get one.

I had what I'd wanted for a long, long time. If Robert decided to relieve me I wouldn't need to work again. All it would take would be a few words about buying the painting spoken like an expert negotiator at the correct time. After buying the painting from sweet Mrs. Camda I was going to definitely indulge myself.

I looked up at the ceiling and saw a huge fly moving back and forth. After a good while it seemed to grow tired of the ceiling and started coming my way. It landed on "Treasure" and as I looked at the absurdly large fly with its huge compound eyes looking at me it took some effort not to piss in my pants.

"Shoo, fly!" I swatted at it with my two-dimensional right arm and it buzzed away; I was grateful that my movements had spared me from the smell of the disgusting thing.

I was a part of the painting as a two-dimensional figure and as a living, breathing human being. Other aspects of the painting such as the steel movie-theater door I'd looked at and which was now only a few feet away from me were three-dimensional right now. The possible ghouls behind the door would be three-dimensional and would have long, sharp fangs—the better to drink my blood with.

The hum of the Exit light was lulling me into a sense of security and there was absolutely nothing wrong with that since I really was secure. I could go behind door # one or wish myself back to the sixty-two year old house and go ahead with my plan.

"I wish that I was back in the bedroom again." I took note of the instantaneous response as I looked around the familiar bedroom of the widowed grandmother. "Treasure" had a slight change in its appearance thanks to my greed. I tapped the pocket which held the diamond and felt at ease.

Food would be nice now. One thing I liked about Robert was the fact that he was reliable. My previous employer could learn a few things from Robert but I really doubted that he ever would.

"Paul? Hey Paul!"

"I'm right here, Robert."

He moved with alarming speed to the bedroom and then stopped as if he'd depressed some internal brake pedal. "I've been looking and waiting for you for over an amazing hour and thirty minutes. Could I be so bold as to ask you where you've been?"

I thought fast. "In the bedroom. In this nice, cozy room admiring the painting on the nice chair. All you had to do was look."

"I looked but I didn't get lucky."

"I really was right here." I nodded and then snapped my fingers. "You're working too hard. I know you've got a lot of stuff to take care of—"

"You're absolutely right. The problem is that I can't take care of things when my employees are jacking off."

"Not guilty, pal. Snap out of it. I'd like for you to know that I've done some really good work today."

"I know. I can smell the paint along with my my own sweat mixed with aftershave. You're not too different from me, young guy. Exactly how much of that cheap fucking cologne do you have on now? The whole bottle?"

I fought to control the laughter which was in me and wanted out. I started to say something and instead of words came the laughter. He was being too funny.

"Hey, Paul. I know I'm funny but that food in the kitchen is nothing to laugh at."

"Burgers, fries, and both are large-sized. Thanks a lot."

"Sure, Mr. Sellers. When you finish with the food I want to talk to you about something."

A raise would be good.

The best burgers came from the cooks at Grillbeef and a sample of their food would seduce practically any vegetarian into the life of a carnivore. The food was very good when one got it from Grillbeef but the extra thirty-odd cents added to the price drove away all but the most appreciative of customers.

"Grillbeef has the competition beat hands down," I said.

"Of course they do. Go ahead and feed your face and stop talking so much."

"Gladly." I walked to the kitchen and sat down, then yanked the helpless food out of the bag and proceeded to wolf the food down like a man who's been denied nourishment for weeks.

What did he want to talk about and what was the "Mr. Sellers" bit about?

I looked back and saw him talking into a cell phone with the force of anger seeming to assist his elocution. As I heard snippets of the conversation I understood exactly what he wanted to talk about.

I didn't sleep with other men's wives unless they were already divorced but Robert probably thought otherwise.

He finished the conversation and came to the kitchen door and then winked at me before his speech. "Have you finished, Paul?"

"Yep." I wiped my lips and face with a napkin. "What can I do for you, buddy?"

"I'm glad you asked that question. Since I don't like people screwing my wife what you can do is to keep your pecker in your pants at all times. This was your last strike, friend. You're almost out."

"That's—"

"Shut up, fucker. You'd better be glad that I'm not whipping your ass right now. I'll bet you want to know who told me. Do you?"

"I really don't because—"

"You'll listen. When I went to pick up the food I ran into Tim."

"And he told you some bullshit lies."

"Not lies, old friend. What you need to do is to get your sorry self out of here quick-like before it's too late." He pulled a cheap cigar out of his shirt pocket, lit it, took a puff, and then exhaled while pointing a thick finger at me. "You're fired as of this second."

"I guess that's it."

"Right, genius. You can get your last check next week." He started tapping his forehead. "Be a good little boy when you pick up your check and don't stay at my office past bedtime."

I was careful to keep the soda in my hand as I got up. I felt my pants pocket to make sure the diamond was still there and when I felt the comfortable lump of carbon I walked to the front door.

I looked at him and noticed that his face had contorted into the look of a very pissed off psychopath.

Fact was I really never had done his wife but the man just didn't want to believe anything except my "guilt". What he didn't know was that my loss of this job really wasn't going to hurt me.

As I looked at the six-one, two-hundred pound bear of a man that had made the decision to fire me I wondered why I'd chosen this type of work.

The pity of all this was the sudden lack of trust.

"You look angry, Robert. For what it's worth—"

"Every second you stand there means the less I can control myself and if I go off—"

"Oh, yeah. I get it. You're a bad-ass. What you'd better not do is jump because if and when you do this young wolf is gonna go into action."

"And they'll take you to jail."

"When they do my lawyer might have something to say about that."

"Take a hike."

"I'm fixing to do that." I rubbed my nose and then grinned for a couple of seconds. "You're a criminally gifted asshole, Robert.

Fuck you very much for hiring me so I could have a shitty little job and just about starve to death."

His psychopathic look of rage diminished a little and I opened the door and walked out into the cruel world with a great chance of making it.

"Treasure", my key to a bright financial future, turned out to be a modestly-priced painting since Mrs. Camda had sold it to me for twenty-five dollars a week after Robert let me go. The guy who'd started buying the rocks from me asked no questions and put cash in my hands instead of talking to me. The green trashbag in my room had a lot of cash in it because of my diamond sales so I called it the "cashbag".

As I prepared for Liza to come to my apartment my thoughts were monotonous in that the single subject was saying the "magic words", getting more loot from the treasure room, and coming back.

Millions of dollars worth of gold, diamonds, and everything else of true significance was mine for the taking. Questions in my mind as to exactly how a painting was able to transport me from a "regular" room into a painting were ones which I needed to subdue for my own greater good.

The doorbell rang and since I was standing right next to it I opened it more quickly and with more force than usual. Liza stood in the light rain and waved at me with two long, thin fingers.

"Can I come in?"

"Of course. Hurry so you don't get wet." She walked in and took off her raincoat and as I shut the door I caught a whiff of her perfume.

"This is definitely a good night for dinner." She ran her fingers through her reddish-blonde hair before smiling and patting me on the back.

"What's on the agenda, Liza?"

"Food, of course."

"You're right."

"Is something wrong, Paul?"

No. I'm just trying to conceal one hell of a hard-on. That's all.

"No." I giggled. "It occurs to me that I met you just a few days ago and we're already hitting it off well."

"I ain't complainin', friend." She licked her lips.

"Me neither."

"You wouldn't mind if I sat down, would you? I want to get comfortable before I eat."

"The kitchen chairs are very comfortable. The meal is called pizza and it's the best kind."

"Great." She rubbed her hands together very fast. "Come here, Paul Sellers. We can sit down and exchange the usual nonsense before the action starts."

"The action?"

"The football game, man. Not the kind of action you might have thought of."

"I wasn't thinking of that."

"Of course you weren't. I'm going to sit down and you can fool with the tube."

"It's been a life-long and not altogether perfect affair with this thing with a gun in it."

"A gun?" She asked.

"Electron gun. I know a little bit about electronics."

"What else do you know about?"

"I was an appliance repairman before I started painting houses."

"Now I'm really going to sit down." She took a seat and folded her arms before giving me a penetrating look. "I'd like to know who you've dated recently."

"I'd really rather not discuss that."

"Fantastic! You passed my test with flying colors, Paul."

"I passed the test with flying colors."

"Right."

"What sort of prize do I get?"

"You'll find out. Look, Paul, I want you to know that if we do anything I'm willing to hang in there with you."

"Marriage?" I asked.

She nodded her head. "I'm tired of being tossed from one asshole to the next. I'll bet if we hooked up it'd last for a lifetime."

"Things are moving real quickly." I smelled the pizza and then checked to see if it was done. "Almost ready. Next time I guarantee you a nice steak with a baked potato and a salad."

"Fine with me, baby. Do you have a Dr. Thirst? I've got a bad taste in my mouth that I want to get rid of."

"Coming up." I opened the refrigerator and pulled out two cold cans of Dr. Thirst and handed one to her.

"Thanks, Paul. This stuff hits the spot." She opened the can and took a long swallow before putting it on the table.

I looked at her and wondered why she wanted to get married.

She might've been aware that I had a lot of cash or she just felt that I'd make a good husband. Other motives such as lust remained a strong possibility but a painful fact remained. The painful fact happened to be that I really didn't want to tie the big knot.

"Enjoying yourself?"

"You bet. I'm glad that you just happened to have my favorite drink." She looked at the wall until her scanning eyes stopped with—"Treasure". "Beautiful! Absolutely great!"

"What's great? Is it me?"

"That painting on the wall is a sight to behold. Where'd you get it?"

"A sweet old lady let me have it for a low, low price. I felt that it was very well worth the money."

"Treasure" had definitely been a modest investment. What she might not want to hear or believe was that it really was a treasure. The question I'd asked myself over and over again was, I judged, part of my possible obsessive-compulsive disorder. The truth about money is something that, to be honest, is the fact that when you have it you have lots and lots of friends. More money means more party and more party sort of leads to mistakes.

"I knew it! You're a rich guy!"

"Not really. I'm between jobs." I went to the refrigerator and got a plateful of cold, boiled eggs and put them on the kitchen table. "Those babies are excellent appetizers. Feel free to indulge yourself."

"I'll wait until dinner."

"What do you want besides pizza?"

"Onion rings." She grabbed my hand and licked it.

"My, my, my. That was different." I fought the urge to respond in a similar fashion.

"We could do something, you know."

I nodded in strong agreement. "That's right. What do you suggest we do to be a great couple? Hmmm? Physical affection really isn't bad at all."

"Get a positive attitude and wear the same clothes that I do."

"Blue jean jacket, loafers, expensive jeans, and a casual shirt."

"I know that you think I'm after you because I licked your hand, Paul."

"I don't mind too much."

As her eyes gleamed she giggled. "Hey, buddy-lovey. I'll bet you've probably had more girlfriends than you can actually count."

"Correct, sweet cheeks." As I looked at the relatively still form of Liza with the slim waist and plentiful bosom my erection was forced to remain rock-hard by willing mechanisms of my body.

"Uh-oh. It looks like you have a problem."

"I do, Liza."

"Smoke a cigarette. That sack in the den's where you keep all of your smokes, I guess. After you puff away I'll try to take care of your problem."

"How thoughtful. Actually, girlfriend, I keep my drugs in that bag."

She looked concerned. "You use drugs?"

"Of course. Only the finest will do."

She rolled her eyes. "Listen, lover, I hate to leave but I'm going to do it anyway."

"So soon?"

"Sorry." She smiled at me in a puppet-like fashion. "I left something at work."

"Okay. Where was that place you said that you work?"

"The Courthouse. We can get together again." She kissed me on the cheek, got up, and then walked to the door with alarming speed before opening it as harshly and efficiently as an incredibly strong man would if he was in the process of rescuing his family from a house fire.

Since she'd left the door open I couldn't help but notice the rain which had increased in intensity and which was in the process of getting the carpet wetter and wetter.

I walked to the door, shut it, and then turned around and looked at the bag on the table.

What exactly had I said to her to cause her to leave? We were talking and she'd asked what was in the sack…and of course the answer was that she must've thought that I had something in the bag as illegal as heroin or the old but reliable cocaine.

A cop friend of hers who stayed close by might be the one who'd probably come to the "rescue" and arrest me. There was a lot of money in the trashbag in my bedroom which the underpaid cop could disseminate and, of course, after my money was seized he'd wind up driving a seventy-five thousand dollar car like all of his newly enriched friends in the precinct. The cop with the forty-caliber gun and the cheap badge was coming and he was coming to take my ass to jail.

In my head I pictured a team of officers who were very trigger-happy and firm in their belief that this single incident would get them promoted. As I examined my mental picture I remembered the supposedly "good" cops and the shit they did to me when I was younger. The image mercifully faded and was replaced by a brainstorming session which sought to find the answer to my current problems. The solution came quickly and I cursed myself for being so feeble-minded.

What I wasn't prepared to do was to explain to the authorities how I'd just happened to come across a magical painting that allowed me inside when I wished for it to happen and which had diamonds that I'd been removing and pawning to an acquaintance. What I was prepared to do was to jump at the opportunity to drink lots and lots of whiskey, preferably Irish whiskey.

"Mr. Sellers, please open the door. I'm with the police and unless you open the door within two minutes I'll be forced to knock it down."

Time to act and act quickly.

I looked at "Treasure" and said: "I wish I was there."

The fair-haired, lanky cop broke down the door. If he would've seen me it wouldn't hurt me since I was in the treasure room but he didn't so I walked to the movie-theater type door and pushed. Nothing happened so I pushed again. The cop was looking around my place and was completely unaware of my own unusual concerns. I pushed again and the door finally opened.

"Mr. Sellers! Come out and talk with me, okay?"

I looked at the huge shape of the cop and then let the door swing shut. There was a time to be thankful and I was particularly thankful enough now and proved it at least to myself by dropping to the floor of this new place and kissing it.

"Thank you, thank you." I looked up at the ceiling. "God, you came through for me again. Thanks, buddy."

I'd stepped into a very long hallway.

As I took in my new surroundings I felt that my escape from the cop might not exactly be the best thing that had ever happened to me because of my new, unique, and weird hangout.

This was my new reality. Although I'd read science fiction when I was younger I'd never actually believed that anything like this could ever happen but it was right in front of me.

I was at the end of a hallway. Across from the door were two vending machines and right next to the door which was two feet away from me sat a padded, comfortable, and blue-colored bench.

I smelled the air which was in between being stale and fresh.

I stepped away from the door and sat down on the bench and noted that the brightly lit hallway still wasn't too bright; the phosphorescent lights on the ceiling radiated the appropriate amount of photons to suit my non-vampiric needs.

No vampires in this hall. What could be waiting for me, though, would be a grinning demon and when I saw him he might begin his evil laughter before escorting me to the Pain Room.

The hall seemed to stretch endlessly with its red carpet and beige-colored walls and ceilings. On the right side of the hall where I was sitting were numerous doors which all looked the same and were spaced, I judged, exactly twenty-five feet from each other.

One good thing about this place just happened to be the temperature and humidity; both were apparently ideal enough for me since I felt quite comfortable.

I caught a whiff of the air again and noticed it smelled like the most expensive and well-kept hotel room money could buy.

Was I in Heaven?

I looked at the vending machines.

Both vending machines had no price, which was good. The snack machine had many offerings to tempt me while the drink machine offered a lot of fruit juices. Both machines carried generic products such as pork skins and grape juice but I didn't care about the lack of brand names.

I got up, got a fruit punch and some pork skins, and sat down again.

The fruit punch came in a one-liter plastic bottle and the skins were enclosed in a large, totally transparent bag. I hadn't had the chance to eat the pizza with my traitor girlfriend but these unburnt offerings would be enough for a good, long while. After this meal I could go back and get a cheeseburger which heated up when shaken briskly.

What was behind all of those doors?

"Let's make a deal, God." I waited for a reply but didn't get one which was obvious to my perception.

I really needed to be concerned about what was behind those doors because I needed a future. I could set up camp in the hall and live off of the vending machine food by day and sleep on the bench at night. All I would then need would be a real good and well equipped bathroom. If the movie-theater type door I'd come through had been a gateway to Hell I should've found out something by now.

I got up and started walking down the hallway.

The first door had the word "Bathroom" painted in white letters on its wooden surface and between it and the next door was a water fountain. I didn't need to do #1 or #2 but I wanted to check out the bathroom. If there was a condom dispenser in the bathroom then most likely they'd be free just like the fruit punch and pork skins I'd obtained from the vending machines.

I stopped in front of the bathroom door and opened it. As I looked I saw a vast bathroom comparable to the bathroom at my local mall where some men grunted and strained to get the last of their turds out before washing their hands and eating chicken with their girlfriends.

I resumed walking and I saw that the next offering was nondescript and rather bland. The room, however, seemed to be drawing me closer sort of like it had a huge magnet which was made to pull humans towards itself rather than metals.

Was it fear, anxiety, or worry that I felt? I wasn't exactly schooled in the field of psychology so I couldn't say what the precise word for my fear was except to say simply that it was fear. Behind all of these doors was the unknown and I had to be the one with huge enough balls to face the music. The thing about my fear was that I could be afraid all I wanted to but if I didn't find out something by opening one of the doors it'd be my loss and I'd have to live with it.

I grabbed the doorknob and opened the conveniently unlocked door.

Ahead of me was a dimly lit room which smelled of cigars, old cologne, and sweat. The only furniture in the room was an ancient desk and two comfortable-looking chairs. On the desk was an ashtray which had a half-smoked stogy in it, two books, and a wireless keyboard.

If Jim Morrison was somewhere in this place I could get him to autograph my syrup-covered napkin. If he was here and I met him face to face then perhaps I needed to question my mental health.

The back of the room had a door that was beginning to open. Suddenly a toilet flushed and the door opened further to reveal a tall, painfully thin young man with uncombed red hair which came down to his shoulders. He grinned and looked at me with green eyes that reminded me of a cat's eyes.

"How's it goin', partner? I'll bet you're thinking that this is some sort of dream and you're gonna wake up in just a minute. Am I right?"

"No, not really. Where the hell am I?"

"Well, pal, it's not only where you are but when."

"Huh?"

"The year thirty-five hundred in a city that used to be called Birmingham, Alabama."

"What's it called now, buddy?" I asked.

"My name's Julius Branson—"

"You painted 'Treasure' like a pro. What do you want?"

"I'll get to that in a few minutes. Let's look at my holographic clock." He touched one of the buttons on his dress shirt and a holographic grandfather clock appeared. "I can make the clock into any style you want and it keeps damned good time if I say to myself."

"I might as well get used to this place."

"That's a good attitude to have, friend." He reached to me and patted me on the shoulder.

"Don't do that. I don't know you and—"

"Of course! It's a macho thing! According to the old-style measurements you're just one-half of an inch taller than six feet while I'm six-seven. We can play basketball." He nodded and then grinned like a wolf. "Basketball still exists, Paul."

"I don't care," I said.

"Technology really has improved a lot since the early twenty-first century. There's an Earth-type planet orbiting an Earth-type star light years from here and, well, I have a condo there."

"Ever since I met you I've noticed you don't always answer questions. Do you have some type of problem?"

He raised his arm and pointed it in my direction and then raised his hand. "Sir, I'm sorry. I know that I might seem evasive but I'm asking you to have patience. Please." He dropped his arm.

"Okay, I will. Just tell me how I got into a painting and what kind of technology was used. Also, Julius, I wonder what you do with all of those diamonds in the Treasure Room. I really want to know."

"Fine, sir. I keep forgetting what people from your time can be like." He walked over to the desk, picked up one book with his left hand and one with his right hand, and then brought them closer so that I could see their titles.

"Alterations in the Space-Time Continuum? A Two-Dimensional Planiverse coexisting with a Three-Dimensional Steriverse? That's a bunch of shit."

"Right. Now explain to me as best you can how you wound up in this painting. Don't be narrow-minded." He started blinking faster.

"Are there others? Why just me?"

"I'll answer that stuff later. Have a seat, man. Relax. We should talk a little bit."

"We should?"

He sighed and then chuckled a little. "It seems obvious to me that you want to know what's in store for yourself. I know I'm not wrong when I say right now, pardner, that you sure don't want to go back to your apartment and have to explain how you managed to get a hundred and seventy-eight thousand dollars in cash."

"How right you are. I'll have a seat."

"Good man." He sat behind the desk and I took a seat in front of it.

"Am I part of some futuristic psychological experiment or something like that? If I am you might as well send me back to my place to deal with the IRS and all of their friends."

"You wouldn't really like for me to do that." He cracked his knuckles and his bohemian-type face looked suddenly serious. "I can assure you that you're definitely not a part of any psychological experiment or, in fact, any experiment."

"If that's the case then why am I here?"

"Good question. The answer is that the Agency needs you to join their ranks."

"What agency?"

"Solse which stands for Solar Security." He laughed again. "It sure sounds like Society Security, huh?"

"I'm losing my patience, Julius. I'll join the fucking agency."

"Consider yourself an agent now because you are one. I don't think you'll feel uncomfortable with any physical combat or anything like that. What you want to know is that the fuckers we're after tried to blow up an antimatter reactor on Mars two weeks ago."

"An antimatter reactor? What about fusion?"

"We still use good old fusion but the big thing for the past three or four-hundred years has been, without question, antimatter power and it really works."

"Sounds something like a show I used to watch."

"I know. We can get you some clothes—"

"Single-breasted. I can give you my measurements."

He shook his head back and forth and then began tapping the desk like it was a drum. "Not necessary. Casual clothes are okay for now."

"You have nice clothes and a nice office. You people sure have come a long way. I kinda wonder why you're here all alone. Don't you have a girlfriend to keep you warm at night?"

He started blinking faster. "I suppose the weirdness of your experience has gotten you a little bit disturbed. Right?"

"Right. You're a true genius when it comes to people."

"Okay, Paul, I'll move on. The pay is good and you'll do whatever is necessary to stop those disturbed souls from hurting anybody, won't you?"

"You can count on that."

"Good." He suddenly seemed to run out of verbal fuel and looked puzzled like a student would when learning Calculus for the first time.

"Is there any kind of test that I have to pass?"

"I'm glad you mentioned that." He cleared his throat.

"Why?"

"I'll show you." He reached for a drawer, opened it, and pulled out a semiautomatic with a silencer already attached. He rubbed it a little like he would if he was fondling his own genitals.

"I'm a good shot," I said.

"Not as good as me." He pointed the gun at me and pulled the trigger three times. I quickly put my hand on my chest to cover my wounds but when I looked seconds later there was no blood.

"Nice toy, huh? You should have seen the look on your face. It was priceless." He started to laugh uncontrollably and in doing so he pushed some internal button in me.

After they fixed his broken nose they shipped me to Mars. Mars has loose women, loose lips, and me to make a difference. All I need now is a cigarette as I pace back and forth thinking about my past. I'm glad they let me quit the Agency after two years to become a full-time artist. "Treasure Two" is my newest masterpiece and I put a lot of work in painting it to perfection. The guy that took my place doesn't like my art but others do. All's well that ends with a good smell from my trusty brush.

ROY'S PLACE

The Quick HC was seconds away so I started slowing the car. I turned right and drove up to one of the pumps. I got out of my car and started walking towards the little store inside where slender, sexy as hell Linda worked.

Linda wasn't available but she might be soon and that made me very comfortable since Tracy had dumped me two weeks ago.

The short walk to the sexy cashier wouldn't be so bad if I didn't have to smell the gasoline fumes which were assaulting me with their funky odor.

I reached the door and it opened automatically thanks to myself and my casual acceptance of technology. I looked and saw no customers and then I noticed Linda behind the plexiglass.

"Roy, get over here before I have to come and drag you over here," Linda said.

"There's no need for any of that." I winked at her. "I could change my mind if the what they call circumstances were right."

"Uh-huh. How much on gas, honey?"

"Ten dollars, sugar. Don't raise the price again."

"It's out of my hands but the scientists are working on something that'll make gas ob-so-lete."

Certainly nothing would make red-headed Linda obsolete for a good while. She'd kept this job for five years and exchanged small talk with me so much that I was used to her. If and when gas became obsolete I could come and fill my car with sugar-water just so I could come and shoot the shit again.

"Money's comin', honey. I have to dig it out of my pocket first." My right hand explored the crowded mini-world of my right pants pocket before finding a ten and handing it to her.

"Appreciate it." She grinned. "When you go back to work Monday I want you to stop here and bring me some of that banana pudding."

"I'll bet you do."

"P-lease, Roy? Don't make me get on my hands and knees."

"Sure. I'll see you later. I'm going to fill up, park, and use the boy's room."

"I hope everything comes out alright." She started to giggle.

"Shush." I left and filled the tank partially with ten dollars worth of high-octane. The place was, I noticed, deserted except for an old truck that a large black man and his white pal sat in while smoking cigarettes. They looked at me and I turned away because I didn't want to start any shit.

Their red truck and its camper-cover revealed nothing to me as to why they were here. The black guy wore a green short-sleeve shirt which didn't cover his huge musculature. The white guy could pass as someone from the British Isles.

Whether or not the two guys had questionable motives was really of no concern to me. Since I didn't want to fill my pants with turds I had no choice but to go to the bathroom and possibly encounter the two men. If robbery happened to be their intent and they robbed me while I was taking a shit they wouldn't leave with green and white stuff but with brown clumpy stuff instead.

I finished putting the gas in, parked my car, and walked to the bathroom. I opened the door and heard the piped-in music of ancient country legends who'd gone to that great bluegrass heaven in the sky. The air conditioning in the bathroom on this hot day was working so well that I felt totally at ease when I opened the toilet door and pulled down my pants before sitting on the overused, slick seat.

My weekend of solitude was really going to be over soon. Tomorrow I'd see my friends at church along with my ex. I'd chosen the life of a cook when I went to trade school and reasoned that since I liked to eat and could eat a lot without getting fat there couldn't be anything better for me to do. Tomorrow I'd go see Dad and he'd tell me again that the insurance business was where it was at and that he'd come to Olsen's with Mom to taste my cooking. A Saturday close to the foothills of the Appalachian Mountains was a Saturday for me to enjoy. Monday, though, was the time to work and see Tracy who'd probably swear that she liked my cooking.

The bathroom door opened and two men—perhaps the two guys—came in.

One had on an enormous pair of work boots and wore jeans while the other one wore average-sized loafers and brown khakis.

I quickened my bowel movement.

"We picked a good time to come here, baby. Two-thousand four in America, Teddy!" The black man giggled.

"Shut up and take a leak. I've got to go too and—"

"That's right. Ni-tro-gen-ous waste. I'll say it again."

"No you won't. I've got to piss as bad as a fucking racehorse."

"Whip it out, Teddy. Whip it out."

"Just for you, faggot." He giggled and the black guy started to giggle.

As I listened to the enormous amounts of urine being emptied into both urinals I smelled the almost overpowering scent of their cologne.

Who were they? I knew they were the two guys and that one was named "Teddy" but the question was really why they were here.

Since I'd never seen them before today it was obvious that they were out-of-staters or out-of-towners.

The sound of urine hitting the urinals ebbed.

"We're gonna launch the missile, man. What target on the Moon do you want me to program it to hit?"

Launch a missile at the Moon? Ah, yes. Escapees from the hospital for the criminally insane.

"Don't worry about it, Quenton. We'll take care of that problem later."

"Whatever you say, boss. Hey, boss, that's our truck out there, isn't it?"

"It sure the hell is. I saw some blond-haired guy about six-three pumping gas out there a few minutes ago. He needs to shave that shit off of his face and get rid of that stupid baseball cap."

I knew they were talking about me but I chose to ignore it.

"Let's get some food, brother. Chili dogs with all—"

"I want to tell you something." He began whispering to his muscle-bound friend.

"Okay, Teddy. I sure got that. Hey! Whoever's using the bathroom better see a doctor because your shit smell really really bad. Don't forget to wipe your ass, mystery man!" He laughed. "Let's get out of here before that funk makes me lose my appetite."

"Of course." He walked the brief distance to the door with his partner, opened the door, and left me to hear it squeak shut.

I wiped, pulled up my pants, zipped them and buttoned them up, and stepped out. As I walked to the sink to wash my hands I could still smell the cologne that one or both of them had liberally applied.

"All I've got to do is be careful about the weird guys. The water of the weird is a strong one." I finished washing my hands and dried them with great haste.

My car was adequate for its purpose. It seemed that foreign cars always seemed to attract people and make them shell out hard-earned dollars. I could protest against the influx of foreign cars except that I myself had shelled out hard-earned dollars for a car which was made in Japan and I was in no way disappointed with it.

I left the bathroom and walked to my car. After I got in I opened a bag of chips and practically inhaled the contents. I started the engine.

The trip home took me down the rural highway for three miles before I turned right and drove up the tree-covered hill that led to my isolated but comfortable home.

I was almost at the house and the conversation of the two disturbed gentlemen started to repeat itself in my brain. I turned into my driveway and forced myself to repress the memory of "Teddy" and "Quenton" so as to enjoy the day I had all to myself. I took the key out of the ignition and got out of the car.

2874 Wilton Drive had been my home for five years, one of which I very definitely had blown trying to keep Tracy from straying too far. It was a modest home and I was an honest, bold, and modest man.

I unlocked the front door and stepped in only to be assaulted by another exclusive report on the radio about President Lake's decision not to run for office again. I chose to do the correct thing and then followed by internal self-programmed decision by walking to the radio and turning the desperate and pathetic program off.

Jim Lake had been a lawyer before he became President and moved from Montana to Washington. I'd voted for him and had been glad about his economic gifts to the country. The thing that needed to be done now was to distance myself as far as possible from politics. My so-called real world was partially empty thanks to Tracy leaving and I needed someone to replace the slut that I'd loved for so long.

I walked to the bedroom, went to my dresser, and then pulled out a neatly folded shirt. As I put it on I caught a whiff of the smelly one that had been the neatly folded shirt's predecessor and gagged.

Being a man means being as great as is possible.

Someone started knocking on the front door.

"Who's there?"

"Linda, Roy. I worked up the courage to come and talk with you."

"I'm comin', baby." I walked to the door and opened it.

"Shit!"

Six-five "Quenton" and five-ten "Teddy" stood right in front of me with guns pointed at my mid-section.

The urinators had come to haunt me.

"Hey, Mister Doo-Doo." He giggled. "What you should have done, Mister Doo-Doo, was look out the window. Is that simple or what?"

"Quenton's right, Mister. In this day and age just about anything bad can happen if one isn't careful enough."

"How—"

"You're referring to when I sounded like your friend." He sighed as if such explanations were beneath him. "It was a device some of my friends put in me before I came here."

"You're not going to get away with this, Ted."

"Your name is—"

"Roy Jansen. I heard you two jokers in the bathroom talking about launching missiles. Which hospital did you escape from?"

"We didn't. Sir, go to our truck and take a peek at the contents in back. I'm sure you might believe us then. If you don't, it's not our loss," Quenton said.

"That makes sense, Quenton, but do I have a choice?"

"The answer is no." Ted made a waving gesture with the gun. "Go and see our little antimatter missile."

I walked to the Detroit masterpiece of a truck followed by Quenton and Ted. I looked through the little window in the camper top to see the missile and some other equipment that I really couldn't figure out so I guessed.

"What do you think?" Ted asked.

"This is so crazy. I was busy enjoying myself and enjoying this nice springtime weather. Why did you bring your shit here?"

"I asked you what you thought."

"The weirdest thing about it, cowboy flunkie."

"And that would be—"

"And that would be a time machine, right?"

"You passed the test. Get your ass inside that house. We've got something special planned for you."

"I'm honored, Ted," I said.

"You should be. Isn't that right, Quenton?"

"Yeah. When we leave let's take some flowers with us."

They didn't know what they were doing and if they did a lot of people were in trouble. I knew that I had a chance and I knew I'd have to kill them. Minutes later I was sitting on the couch sipping a glass of ice water which Ted had been "kind" enough to provide. Quenton was watching a history program while Ted smoked a cigarette that he'd bought from the station or so he told me.

"Roy?"

"What is it, Quenton?"

"Don't you agree that Hitler was an asshole?"

"For all intents and purposes, yes."

"Switching the subject, Roy. This green shirt, I have to admit, shows off my muscles very tastefully."

"What do you want?" I asked.

"It has something to do with a court case, doesn't it Ted?" Quenton winked at him.

"Right. The time we come from is filled with injustice. Murderers such as ourselves actually get executed in the year twenty-five hundred more than this year in the early twenty-first century.

Those assholes on the Supreme Court turned down our cases," Ted said.

"What exactly did you two do?" I sipped some of my water.

"Murder, rape, blew up a few buildings. One thing I'm glad I did a few weeks ago was to see Freddy Dangerous. I like punk rock. My partner wanted to go to Vegas and win some money with his sure-fire techniques but we've run into you and we have to do something about it. I just wanted to see Freddy before he committed suicide."

"He's gonna kill himself?"

"Yep. This place is so nice," Ted said.

"Of course you're not serious about blowing up the Moon."

"Actually we are."

"That's not right."

"You might have a point, Roy. Is it right for a cop to kill your father? No, of course not. But that's actually what some cop son of a bitch did. What it is is that I don't really want to blow the Moon or anything else for that matter but I have to," Ted said.

"I don't think you have to."

"But we do, Roy," Quenton said.

"Let me have some of that cologne that you both wear. It smells great."

"Of course. Want a cigarette, too?"

"I'll just take the cologne, Quenton."

"As you wish." He pulled a small bottle out of his pocket and handed it to me.

"Thanks." I waited for the chance to use my fighting skills on the two delusional psychopaths with pleasure.

"What do you actually do for a living?" Quenton looked at me and his face told the story of a confused and puzzled man.

"Both of you should come over here and sit with me. I guarantee right now that I won't do anything stupid." I looked at Quenton holding his gun and Ted holding his in his left hand. Their grips seemed loose.

"Hey Ted," Quenton said.

"Yeah?"

"Roy wants to kill us. Roy, from what I understand you can't cook worth a shit. I've heard rumors that you play with your ass before you fix a meal. If that's true, Doo-Doo, then how the hell do you plan to keep on working with a clear conscience?" Quenton asked.

Sweat was trickling down the right side of Ted's face and he stared at me with blue eyes that had originated in the future. Since that's what they wanted me to believe I chose not to. I concentrated on the hum of the kitchen freezer and then on Quenton's white-toothed smile.

They definitely needed their asses kicked and I was ready for the job. Despite my acknowledgment of the possibility that fate was punishing me for a near-perfect and carefree life there was no need to give up.

"Quenton, friend, you shouldn't have said that," I said.

"Is it true, Roy? Is it true that you want to kill us? That breaks my heart." Ted's face sagged like someone I'd seen in an old black and white movie before he farted. "Shame on you, Roy."

"There there, Ted. Don't let that perplexing pistol-whipping pugilist hurt your feelings. We might need to punish him with our pistols," Quenton said.

"It'd at least end the suspense, crazy fucker," I said.

"The suspense of what?"

"You and your friend really aren't from the future and when they lock you up again you won't get out."

"I'll choose to ignore what you just said with my boss's permission."

"You've got it," said Ted.

"Okay. I'm going to go in the kitchen and get something for all three of us to eat," said Quenton.

"I've got some candy bars on the counter and cold sodas in the fridge."

"Not very nutritious but it'll have to do. I'll be back in a few seconds." He got up and walked to the kitchen.

The play for whipping their butts should start when Quenton came back with the food.

"Ted, why do you want to blow up the Moon?" I giggled a little.

"The United States of the future is good for some. We have starships exploring distant parts of the galaxy, we have fusion power, we have everything. Everything except justice. When I screwed her she said she wanted it and when she started hitting me I had to fight back or I'd be the one that was killed instead of her. I'm going to take care of the problem by shooting the missile at Mare Tranquillitatis and then me and my friend'll leave before—"

"Candy bars and sodas. What a wonderful junk-food combination." Quenton walked in with three sodas and six candy bars which were contained in one of my old plastic grocery bags.

"Gosh, Quenton, I'm so grateful," I said.

"I'm sure you are. Ted, grab a candy bar and a soda. They're chilled." Quenton handed him the bag. Ted got his and the Quenton walked up to me and loomed over both myself and the couch.

I slapped the couch. "I'm going to redden your mustache."

Quenton appeared dumbfounded. "Pardon?"

"I said I'm going to redden your mustache." I tripped him and he fell down like a large tree. Ted was about to put a bullet in me so I stopped him by kicking the gun out of his hand. It didn't discharge at all so, emboldened with my success, I kicked Ted's legs and punched him in the eye with a little extra effort.

"You son of a bitch!" Ted shouted.

"Want some more, Ted? Huh?" I started to swing when huge hands grabbed me from behind. I managed to break free and hit Quenton in the mouth. I started to swing again but Ted knocked me down from behind.

"My lips are bleeding, Roy. That wasn't very nice attacking us like that." To punctuate his statements Quenton used my head as a football and kicked it.

Why did the motherfucker kick me in the head?

"Mister, you're in trouble. Turn him over, Quenton. I'm going to have to kill our new friend."

"I will." Giant hands turned me face-up and I stared into the barrel of Quenton's nine-millimeter.

"Shoot, motherfucker!! Shoot!"

"You got it." Quenton started or appeared to be obeying my order by slowly pulling the trigger but no bullet issued from the barrel. He grinned. "Darn it, Roy. I forgot to load my clip. Will you forgive me just this one time?"

"This is so stupid. Yes, Quenton, I forgive you."

"I should be the one to take the life of the Southern gentleman. He gave me a black eye and for that he needs to be promptly shot," Ted said.

"There's no need, boss. I can put the Belt around his neck. When the Moon blows up he'll sit, unable to move, and watch as his whole life gets fucked up."

Ted was silent for several seconds and appeared to be totally lost in thought. "Get it. And while you're at it get me another pack of my cigarettes from the carton."

"What the hell's the belt?" I asked.

"Something that I'm going to wrap around your neck. It prevents any hostile physical movements by interfering with motor nerve neurotransmitters. You've got to learn not to hurt people," Quenton said.

"Apparently both of you have already failed that test. What if I want to drink a glass of milk with the 'Belt' on?"

"It prevents hostile movements, dumbass. You can still drink a stupid fucking glass of milk," Ted said.

"Let me ask you a question, Quenton," I said.

"Make it quick, baby. I gotta get the equipment ready."

"What would you do if you were in my position?"

"Probably attempt to subdue me and Ted." He sniffed and then feebly pointed at me. "The thing about it, though, is that I'm not you."

"And you should be glad. Some pathetic country bumpkin who cooks for a living—"

"Shut your fucking mouth, Ted. I don't want to hear that shit."

"You're lucky that Quenton is your friend."

"I don't want that kind of luck. Both of you need to go back to the hospital—"

"We're not from a hospital. Anyway, Roy, you're fighting days are over with. Isn't that right, Quenton?"

"Damn straight." Quenton started laughing and Ted joined in.

When it appears that your losing, use all strategies. There was no need for me to quit. Negotiation was a very palatable strategy.

Thirty minutes later I had the "Belt" around my neck and it was like a blood pressure cuff only not as tight.

It was time to manipulate and negotiate.

"Cigarette?" Ted held out one in an attempt to soothe me or so it seemed.

"No thanks."

"This house is tastefully decorated. All the colors are placed appropriately and it smells good in here. Can I look at the newspaper?"

"I can't stop you, Ted."

"I was trying to be polite."

"Try to be something else, short stuff. Really what you need to do is to try to be something in place of the asshole you've always been."

"I choose to ignore that comment."

"Okay. Quenton, get your ass out of my bathroom now!"

"You aren't making it easy on yourself! As you should know, Roy, a man has the God-given right to take a shit when nature calls."

This was turning into a bathroom kidnapping. The endlessly functioning bladders and bowels could have their contents substituted with lemonade and chocolate pudding without any complaint from me. All that was necessary now was for me to hit myself in the head to dislodge the fecal material trapped within so that I could escape from this pathetic nightmare.

The toilet flushed. The outside heat combined with the recent rains allowed me to hear the expansion joints do their duty. Ted and Quenton didn't need to add their own sounds to my house yet they had and still were.

"Rough stuff. You made me come out too soon, Roy boy."

"Everything come out okay?"

"Almost." He reached into his pocket and dropped a turd on my lap while blinking very fast.

"Get this fucking thing off of me!"

He started laughing and Ted joined in. After twelve minutes Ted had partially lost control of his bladder and the laughing stopped. Quenton wiped tears from his face.

"Quenton, you should have been a comedian." Ted said.

"I act, therefore I am. Sorry about that little plastic turd, Roy."

"I'll bet you are."

Quenton looked at Ted. "Tomorrow in his back yard."

"Yes. Roy, you have the good or probably according to you the bad fortune of having your back yard be the host of my little missile launcher. We're going to spend the night here and after we launch that missile tomorrow you can kiss your ass goodbye."

"What do you expect me to say?" I asked.

"Hurl curses at us. Threaten. Anything."

"That won't accomplish anything at all, Ted, and you know it."

"True. What do you have in mind?" Ted asked.

"A deal."

Quenton laughed. "Psychology, huh? You people sit around and watch so much T.V. that in your weak freak minds you become negotiators that get the bad guys in trouble. This isn't a television show, Roy. Not everything ends well, you know."

"This is a genuine offer that I'm talking about."

"Continue, Roy. I want to hear it all," Ted said.

"How shall I put it?"

"Any way you want to, blond white man," Quenton said.

"Okay. I want to be a partner. I want to join your team."

"What do you have to offer us?" Ted asked.

"I'm a good cook and I know a lot of history. It's my hobby."

"He might be good. What do you think, Ted? Should we let this joker join us?"

"Sure."

Quenton extended his hand and I shook it. "Welcome to the club, Roy." He looked at my lap. "Do you like that dog turd on your lap? The fake ones are always best for some reason. Do you?"

I looked down. "Of course not." I flipped it with my middle finger and it fell to the floor, subtracting from my beige carpet's beauty.

"We'll take the Belt off in a couple of minutes. One thing I have to tell you, Roy, is that I don't like the court system in this country. It's even worse in the time we come from."

Quenton looked serious and hurt. "The motherfuckers turned down our appeals. All we did was make a few little mistakes."

"A lot of big mistakes, actually. They still had no right," Ted said.

"Roy, Roy. What crimes have you ever committed?" Quenton asked.

"Smoked a few joints in school. Said 'fuck you' to my Dad."

"Have you ever, in your entire life, killed a man?" Ted asked.

"No. I'm tired of being questioned."

"We're sex offenders, aren't we Ted?"

"That we are."

"I'll bet you're lonely, Roy. A kind man like myself could provide you with the love and comfort you need." He fell silent and Ted did too. Quenton started staring at me, got up from his chair next to Ted's, and began to walk slowly towards with with his hands extended.

"You better stop that shit now, Quenton! If you jump and I ever get loose—"

Quenton howled with laughter while Ted took the role of the straight man who knew nothing, nothing, and exactly nothing.

"Very funny. Take this Belt off my neck."

Quenton shut his laughter off like one would turn a light off. The look of fake remorse added fuel to fire of my irritation with the man. He cleared his throat. "Hey, buddy. I-can't-do-that. I sure as hell wasn't born yesterday, amigo. But I've got to hand it to you, Roy. I really do. Nice try."

"I haven't seen the missile you say you have or the time machine either," I said.

"Both are in our truck. You'll get to see the missile tomorrow," Ted said.

"How long will it take the missile to get to the target?" I asked.

Ted ran his right hand through his brown hair. "Ten minutes. It could go faster but my partner and I need time to escape to a parallel future. You don't mind if I help myself to some coffee, do you? Of course you don't."

"Fix us those microwave frozen dinners, too. Roy-boy?" Quenton said.

"Yeah?"

"Wanna eat?"

Not as bad as I want to put both of you six feet under.

"Certainly. Fix me a frozen dinner, Ted. Iced tea would be good too."

"I'll fix the food. Roy, I really want to kill you. The only reason I haven't is that the destruction of the Moon and its effects on Earth will be even more dreadful for you." Ted said.

"And if your time machine doesn't work you'll wind up dead too, Ted."

"It won't."

"Are you sure, asshole?"

"Quite." He rose to his full five-ten height and headed for the kitchen.

"Time for you to start praying, Roy," Quenton said.

"No. There's no need to because both of you have very serious delusions that you've come from the future and have a missile which you're going to use to blow up the Moon. Show me something I can work with."

"I did, Roy. I put down my gun. That's a sign of peace."

"That was a choice that both of you made and there's no proof that you came from the future. There is evidence that both of you are—"

"Okay, Roy the Skeptic." He pulled a small computer out of his pocket and pressed a button. "Complete blueprints of a fusion reactor."

"Turn off the T.V., Quenton. The sound's been off for hours and there's no use running up my power bill."

He patted his slender waist. "I'll do it in a flash, Doo-Doo."

Quenton tapped the remote and I felt better not having to look at the caffeine-enhanced news anchor deliver more bad news. "Thanks."

"You're welcome. Drink some of your water and I'll show you the way most of us get electricity in the future."

"I'm not thirsty and I don't believe you."

"Well well well." A fatherly I-told-you-so look replaced his comedic countenance. "Don't believe me. Instead believe in what happens tomorrow as an example of technology becoming too advanced."

"I hope Ted's going to gain some weight with my food," I said.

"You changed the subject."

"That's my perogative, muscles."

"You're not going to make it. Your entire life's been a joke and the punch line comes tomorrow. You're a loser, Roy. A loser with a heart of gold. I'll remember you after I leave."

"I can still kick your ass, you know."

"Of course you can, Roy. But that won't be true much longer."

Food didn't succeed in satiating my appetite because the emphasis within me was on survival. Since I didn't succeed in spilling drink on Ted's dress shirt thanks to the Belt I went through the motions and let sleep take over.

I woke up and noticed the draft in the house along with the songs of birds. As I scanned my living room I noticed that I was the only person in the room. "Quenton? Ted? Tell me that I'll be able to enjoy this fresh air without worrying that you'll shoot off your play missile today, okay?"

My life really hadn't been a joke but instead it had been fun. Maybe I could play some more basketball with my friends after the sheriff took my two new friends back to the hospital where they belonged. If what they claimed was true I was in trouble and as far as the Belt was concerned it obviously belonged to the government lab that Ted or Quenton or both of them had stolen from. There was no way lives could be taken by a missile Ted had dreamed up after reading perhaps dozens of thick science fiction novels.

All I needed was a chance. Just one.

Quenton came into the living room without any obvious expression on his face. He moved closer and closer to me while his gun was pointed directly at my head.

"Is something wrong, Quenton?"

"You're damned right something's wrong. It's a bad thing that you don't have a cell phone since Ted cut your phone line but don't worry."

"Why? Since I'm all helpless with this thing around my neck you can give in to your homosexual tendencies and fuck me up the ass."

"I'm a cop. Undercover cop. How very unfortunate that your closest neighbors are two-hundred and fifty yards away."

"Use your future version of a phone and call the local police. I wouldn't complain."

"No can do, cowboy. I'm going to take care of this with your help if that's okay with you."

"Sure. Where's Ted?"

"In your back yard trying to decide when to launch the missile." He giggled. "What that poor, stupid man doesn't know is that not only did I disable the missile but I also replaced all of his ammunition with blanks. It's over and he's lost."

"So you'll kill him with your laser."

"We didn't bring those types of weapons with us although I could construct one. You get to kill Ted."

"It's that easy, huh? You took me hostage and you now expect me to believe that you're an undercover cop in addition to believing your delusions about the future."

"Believe what you want. You can go ahead and kill him if you wish, Roy."

"Sure. Take this fucking thing off of my neck."

"With pleasure." He put the gun in his left hand and removed the Belt from my neck with alarming speed and precision.

"The first thing I'm going to do to thank you for taking that thing off of my neck is going to be whipping your protruding ass, fucker-upper." I rose from the couch like a corpse that's just escaped the confines of a grave.

He grabbed my arm before I could throw any punches. "I know that you're upset but save it for later. We'll go out there, he'll attempt to kill us both with his blanks, and he'll fail at which time I'll either arrest him or one of us'll have to put him out of his misery."

"Okay, Superrooper cop. Do I get the gun?"

He handed it to me. "Don't use it unless you have to, Mr. Jansen."

"I'll be sure to keep that in mind."

"There's a reason for everything."

"And?"

"I don't know. My old lady told me I should get a better job. She knew, absolutely and without a doubt, that shit like this would happen and that when it did she might lose a husband."

"Don't cry over spilled milk, Quent." I smiled and stared at him. "I could personally take care of that dog turd for you right now. If he dies it won't be a great loss, will it?"

He shook his head no and walked to the kitchen. Since my legs were awake I could follow him so I did.

"Eat something and chase it with something cold. Don't starve."

"If you insist, Quenton." I poured myself a glass of orange juice, took a few bites off of a cold but still edible sausage biscuit, then congratulated myself for my will to keep my cool in unreal situations like the one currently taking place.

"Hurry up, Roy. You've got to see this."

"I can already see that it's another nice Spring day." I cleared my throat. "When I said you were a Superrooper cop I was talking gibberish; Superrooper wasn't the word I meant to say."

He smiled like a wolf who'd just run into good luck. "What was it then, Roy?"

"Superstupid. Why? Because you might not have done a good enough job disabling that missile and if he launches it—"

"He could simply launch it by voice command. It won't work, though he might have thought about it for awhile and since he's the paranoid type he might've figured out that I was a cop."

"Gosh, Quenton. That makes me feel so safe."

"The fuck-ing miss-ile won't work, white man. How many ways are there to explain it?"

"I believe you."

"Good. Real good. Chum on over here to the window in this nice kitchen of yours. Chum on."

I obeyed and when I got to the window a glance at Quenton's face gave me the impression that he was hopelessly trapped in a psychopathic fantasy that knew no bounds.

He pointed to Ted who was outside relaxing. "Look at that pig."

"At least he's enjoying himself. In fact he looks ready."

"For what?"

"For us to come out there and mess up his revenge. Terrible."

"Look at that missile launcher. It's a masterpiece," Quenton said.

The missile launcher was a long tube which rested on a fairly thick metallic disk. Attached to the bottom of the disk were robotic legs which most likely moved the missile launcher to different locations and ingeniously took the place of wheels.

The missile tip poked out of the tube by at least half a foot or more. I looked at it from every angle I possibly could since even though its payload could destroy the Moon and possibly the Earth it was a masterpiece just as Quenton had said. The legs on the launcher got out of their squatting position and began to walk towards Ted who appeared quite comfortable in my lawn chair.

"He ain't gonna blow anything up," I said.

"Correct opinion, cook."

"Why didn't you arrest that man in my back yard weeks ago? Were you scared? I get it, though. He was the one crazy enough to blow up the Moon and you went along for the ride. Answer the question. Why?"

"Because he had to do certain things first. The time-tourist business has to be cleansed of people like Ted Kelly. In the time I come from everything is progressing quite well. When problems like Ted come up they look to guys like me for the solution."

"The solution is obvious. I might even sweat a salvo of bullets."

"Roy, Roy! He has to do something!"

"I'm going to walk out this door and if his gun doesn't have blanks and he manages to shoot me I'm going to make sure that I take out at least you before I die. Understand?"

"Be appropriate. I'm coming out in a few seconds too."

"Have anything to say before I go out there?"

"The instant you start to go out the back door have your gun ready to fire." He looked at the weapon I held with my right hand. "The safety's off and that's good. You have my permission to kill him."

"What'll it be? What about arresting him? You need to make up your mind, Quenton."

"Kill the crazy son of a bitch. He's capable of lots of things and I think you should put an end to his talents by putting a bullet in his overdeveloped brain."

"I might just do that." I pulled the door open slowly, pushed the screen door open gently, then let it close softly before putting my shoes on the steps.

I'd never killed a man but my tempter who said he'd be right behind me seemed to want me to put an end to the life of the man sitting in my lawn chair.

He was fifteen feet away from me with his back turned.

Why was he so calm?

I advanced on him like a man who's about to assassinate a terrible leader and noticed that either he was pretending not to hear me or he was hard of hearing. I also noticed that his gun was on my grass which now had several large indentations from the walking missile launcher.

"Roy, honey, I wouldn't do that if I were you," Ted said.

"Unnecessary use of your voice duplicator isn't the best strategy and I'm damned sure that I'm not going to fall for that cheap trick again," I said.

"Of course you won't. It was—"

"Try tossing that gun you have over to me."

"If I don't?"

"I'll shoot you."

"Shucks. Here it is." He got up very fast, picked up the gun, and tossed it to me.

"It wouldn't have done you much good. Quenton put blanks in it."

"You almost lost, Roy."

"Almost doesn't count now."

Quenton came out of the house and stepped over to where I was. "I was listening to your conversation and Roy's right. Almost really doesn't count. Do your duty, Roy. Shoot that piece of shit."

"Is this really necessary?" I asked.

"Give me the gun, Roy," Quenton said.

"I don't think—"

"Give me the motherfucking gun!"

I handed it to him.

"Quenton Traddell. How did you ever figure out I was a cop?" Ted asked.

"You've known me long enough to know that I'm not stupid, Ted. I really have to hand it to you, though." He waved the gun in a circular pattern before pointing the gun in the general direction of both Ted and me. "You ain't going to make it, punk cop. When I go to the parallel Atlanta or whatever it is those scientists call it I'm going to be a true king whereas cops like yourself and losers will be mine to deal with however I please."

"How do I fit into the equation?" I asked.

"He's going to kill you," Ted said.

"Right. Very good." He turned his head and coughed. "I'm also going to kill *you*, Ted. By the way, Roy, I didn't disable the missile."

"I suppose I have a chance at beating you," Ted said.

"Blanks against live rounds. That sounds marvelous. Roy and Ted, you need to stand to the left of the missile platform. Do it now or both of you die. You each have a total of ten seconds to get there. Ten seconds, nine, eight, seven—"

I moved to the left of the platform and looked at my trees and Ted followed me with a superhuman feat of speed.

"Quenton, this is ridiculous," Ted said.

"Wrong, wadwaste." He picked up the gun with blanks and tossed it over to a spot of grass next to Ted's feet. "Pick it up, Teddy."

Ted did as he was told.

"If you lose—"

"I won't, Roy. It's just one of those things that happens." He started giggling. "Do you like your nice, comfortable house?"

"You bet your ass I do."

"I don't. You won't be needing it anymore, cook." He pulled a black sphere out of his pocket that was slightly smaller than a grenade, pressed a button on it, and tossed it towards my window without taking his eyes off of me. The object crashed through my window and I heard a muted explosion which was followed by flames which seemed to instantly engulf my kitchen.

"That was real low, Quenton. You don't burn a man's house down like that and expect to get away with it," I said.

"But I just did. Tell you what, boys. I'm going to start another countdown. I'm going to tell that launcher to fire the missile at the preselected target on the Moon. I'll give someone the chance to kill me and—"

"The blanks'll give you a heart attack?" I asked.

"That was a good one, Roy. Just because you offered that bit of humor you're going to be the one that pulls the trigger. I'll tell the launch computer to fire one minute after I say start. You'll get to fire the first shot, Roy."

"When the three minutes are up? You're so kind and generous I have to force the vomit to stay in my mouth."

"Do that, Roy. Ted, give Mr. Jansen your gun."

"I don't think—"

"I know that you don't think. Give him the gun or I'll drop you and do it myself."

Ted gave me the gun.

Goodbye, life.

"This isn't fair, Quent," I said.

"Of course not. Life isn't fair either but you have to go along with the game." He groped for something in his pocket and pulled out a stick of chewing gum.

"Put it in your mouth. While you're chewing you might forget the methods you have to use to be an asshole," I said.

"That's impossible," Quenton said.

"I rest my case."

"Very fucking funny. Are you ready?"

"Yep," I said.

"Don't do it, Quenton. The man didn't bother you at all."

"Roy, tell your friend to keep his mouth shut. Tell him!"

I looked at Ted. "Better keep quiet, Ted. He might change his mind in a few seconds."

"Not likely. Before I kill you, Roy, I want you to know that I've enjoyed your company and sense of humor."

I looked at his sweat-drenched shirt. "Are you hot?"

"Yes. One of the things about having a gifted criminal mind like the one I have is that it works best when cool. Something like a computer except that I don't have a fan. Anyway, Roy Doo-Doo, here goes. Computer, launch missile not in three minutes like my confused friend said but one minute after I say start. Start."

I aimed at his heart for all the good it did me.

"You feel unlust, of course, but you'll die real quick."

"There's an afterlife, Quenton. I'm really not worried."

"For your sake I hope so." He looked at the green digital readout on the side of the disk which said fifteen seconds were left.

"When I say fire you pull the trigger. It'll be five seconds from now. Three, two, one, fire!!!"

I pulled the trigger and the gun recoiled like a cannon. Smoke came out of the barrel too fast, and I looked up to see Quenton. He fell to his knees with a look of surprised horror and gratitude. He put his right hand on his ruined chest in a valiant but useless attempt to stop the flood of blood.

"Shit! I thought you put blanks in the gun, you big fool!"

He looked at me and managed to smile. "That wasn't very nice, Roy. Enjoy your life." He fell face first into the grass and apparently died the good way.

"You don't see any missile firing, huh?"

"No, Ted. How'd you do it?"

"It can summed up by me saying that in my line of work I take nothing for granted and I always think about possibilities." He reached into his pocket and pulled out a packet of what looked like cocaine and threw it down next to the now dead and huge rascal of a man that I'd come to know and dislike.

"Cocaine? What the hell are you doing?"

"They'll want to know what happened. They can, of course, come up with a few theories."

"I can tell the police what happened. I can—"

"That's right. You don't want to stay here with a burned down house and a dead man on your grass."

I looked at my nearly destroyed house, smelled the smoke, and heard the approaching law enforcement and safety vehicles coming my way. Neighbors had ventured out of their homes and I could see them pointing in my direction.

Reality was right here, right now. Really my future lay in the distant future.

"What needs to be done?" I asked.

"All I have to do is get the launcher in the truck and activate the negative energy. We'll go through the wormhole and you'll spend the rest of your life in the future."

"I'm accustomed to doing that."

"You just passed the test."

"That's great. I can come back to see my mother, father, and—"

"Yes."

"Good, Ted. Listen here. There's a man who's staining my grass with his blood because he was crazy as shit and wanted to hurt people. Are you any different?"

"I think so. I've got some chicken in the truck. We can eat it while we take a little trip."

"Fried?"

"Sure."

"Let's go."

"You have anything cold to drink?"

"Cola. Listen, Roy, I have to tell you something."

"Go ahead."

"I'm not a cop, but the people I work for are going to pay me a lot of money when I get back. Quenton really was a cop before he went bad. When he went bad he"—Ted whooshed—"what he did was rape his brother's wife."

"That's lowdown."

"There's more, Roy."

"I might as well hear it."

"He wasn't satisfied with just raping her. After he raped her he took her head off with a shotgun before killing her three little kids."

"Why didn't he use a ray gun or something like that? Aren't you folks a little ahead of shotguns?"

"We sure are. The point is that the man staining your grass was very, very bad."

"Not anymore. Let's take that trip, Ted. I'm ready for the chicken right now," I said.

"Okay. You can work for me, you know."

"I know." I took a last look at my place and then left with Ted.

INVESTMENT

I wiped the tears from my face which seemed to not want to stop coming from my eyes.

Since Ellen killed herself and ruined my wedding plans I'd been inclined to bury myself in work and today was one of the days when it really wasn't necessary to be so intense.

As I picked up my glass of root beer and took a few swallows I made a mental note which said that this should be a good day and with me good days were truly unique.

I looked at the new Byte computer that I'd bought two days ago.

I'd sold my old computer and used the money for groceries. The salesman that had pitched my old bucket of circuitry wasn't as good or as truthful as the one who'd sold me my newest tech toy.

I sipped some more root beer.

The salesman who'd pointed out my new PC had enthusiastically informed me that new advances in photolithography had allowed an incredible number of transistors to be put with precision into the computer's processor. The computer had everything. He'd told me that it was the best one that money could buy and I agreed with him and knew through both intuition and wishful thinking that I'd made the right decision. The new computer was the king shit of computers.

"Come back, Ellen!" I got up and put the root beer on the dresser and then sat back down.

The guy that convinced me to buy the computer had joked that it had been taken from a government base where flying saucers were kept and that if I revealed that the computer was really a product of reverse engineering I'd be in a heap of trouble. The story was laughable but it still wasn't a bad idea if someone such as myself chose to use it as the plot of a cheap science fiction novel.

The computer would fit in nicely for the type of work I was in. After I tested it out at the store before buying it parting with nine-hundred dollars had never seemed as cost-effective and wise. I needed to get started on my third novel and test out the word processor again although I knew it worked. If I wrote another article it would be a quick thousand for me and it would be the good money that paid for the computer's expense. A bestseller would emerge from both myself and the electronic masterpiece. There was no room for failure.

I had some tricks that I used to motivate myself to think up ideas quickly. One of them was to eat a plateful of lasagna with garlic bread and a salad. Another one recently added was to fantasize that Ellen and I were living in marital bliss in a mansion that had been purchased thanks to my extra large royalty checks. What really and truly did the trick, though, was smoking a genuine non-menthol cigarette.

"Time to light up," I said. I looked at the pack of Slams on the desk next to the computer. They didn't look offensive so I pulled one out of the pack, lit it, and inhaled. I began to feel the great rush that I liked so much. I tapped ashes onto the ancient ashtray.

The computer smelled just as good if not better than a new car.

As I smelled it I knew it was time to come up with a good idea.

I turned it on and double-clicked the word processor icon. When the word processor popped up I went to my blank idea file and typed: Missiles are being installed in Cuba with the help of foreign advisers. Missiles will be launched October 26, 2005 at precisely 4:30 P.M. I clicked on Save and then promptly and without hesitation turned off the computer so that the electronic components could take their nap.

My stomach began to protest its emptiness.

Fast Food Chef was just the right restaurant for me. The place had started in Alabama and now had several locations scattered across the southern United States.

I mentally noted that my appetite for junk food was reaching almost dangerous territory but actually I still didn't care.

The cigarette had come to the end of its short life so I put it out and picked up the car keys which were next to the computer.

I had enough for my munchies which was very, very good.

I walked to the front door, opened it, walked out and locked it, then strolled to my car and took a seat. As I put the key in and started the engine I knew that I had to include onion rings with the order or I'd be hungry again. While my guts did their usual tricks I drove the V6 job under the speed limit to satisfy my insatiable hunger.

I was getting close to the nearest Fast Food Chef.

I looked at the familiar blue and white sign before making the right turn. Getting in line quickly and grateful that there were only a few cars in the drive-through area I mentally prepared to order.

This was the time for some good hot dogs.

The driver ahead of me finished ordering and advanced forward. I pulled up next to the microphone and when I rolled down my window I was greeted by a pleasant fall breeze.

Ellen, I wish you were here right now.

As I prepared to state my demands to the minimum-wage All American girl my hunger grew slightly more intense.

"Welcome to Fast Food Chef. May I take your order?"

"I'll take the Chef Special #1. And let me have some sauerkraut with the order." My mouth was watering. I thanked the entire restaurant chain that #1 included onion rings.

"Thank you. That'll be four seventy-eight."

I drove to the window and paid her. When she handed me the food I temporarily forgot my manners and snatched it from her hands. The smile she had was quickly replaced by a look of mild irritation. I drove away and was careful about the root beer since I didn't want it to spill. I put the first hog dog in my mouth as I left the parking lot.

The possibility of me having a good day existed. What it probably depended on was me. Ellen was no longer available to talk to but there had to be a way for me to start again. Once you become an expert at something then undoubtedly there are plenty of reasons to enjoy life but still life holds no guarantees. It does, however, offer possibilities.

I was almost home.

I looked and saw a police car parked in front of my house.

Why?

One tall, lone officer stood in my driveway with a grin on his thin face.

I stopped in front of my house and got out of the car. I then moved closer to him until he was about three feet away and then stopped.

If I'd broken the law it might be the last time.

"Can I help you, officer?" As I looked his grin seemed to turn into an evil, ass-kicking grin that I'd seen in an old action movie.

"Well sir, that depends on who you are. Is your name Lester Jones, partner?"

"Yeah. Something happen?"

He adjusted his sunglasses. "I'm sorry to have to tell you this, Mr. Jones, but you're under arrest."

"This might sound funny but I've got to ask."

"Ask away, sir." He wiped a single drop of sweat from his cheek.

"Why?"

"I think you know the answer to that question."

"I can straighten this out. I really can."

"This is just a suggestion, Lester, but next time pay your fines so that we don't have to come here and take you to the lodge."

"I knew that I forgot something. I knew it!"

"I'll bet you'll remember next time."

"You're right." I offered my hands to be cuffed.

"Sorry, sir." He handcuffed me and I got in the back seat of the squad car and waited to get to jail to call my lawyer.

Philip told me to do my short time and then pay the fines.

The jail was a place where I would grow as a writer. Yes indeed.

One person shared my cell with me. He was an olive-skinned businessman who stood about six-one and must have weighed two-hundred pounds even. They said he liked to fight but he didn't bother me at all. I really wanted to know his name.

The monotonous view of the cell and its contents remained a constant except for the occasional guard or jailed citizen that passed by.

As I looked at the departing floor-mopper I summoned forth my courage which had been made at least slightly more powerful thanks to the eggs, grits, and toast I'd eaten earlier.

Courage was what I'd used to win friends and make myself into a person who lived rather than just simply existed.

"What's your name?" I asked.

I looked across at him.

On the steel table in front of me was a crossword puzzle which had been torn out. The rest of the newspaper was scattered on the table in an orderly fashion with a pen sitting neatly on top of the sports section. The entire puzzle was completed. Apparently he had a fairly good mind.

I pulled my elbows off the table and sighed. It seemed as if every morning when I woke up there was always something new and interesting.

"I wonder what took you so long," he said.

"Say again?" I cracked my knuckles while glancing at my copy of Crime magazine which lay on top of my bedsheet before returning my attention to my new friend who honestly seemed competent enough to be a prosperous businessman.

"You waited a long time to ask my name. Why?"

"I didn't feel like it was that important."

"Good enough reason, friend."

"And your name just happens to be—"

"John Garcia, Lester. I prefer John instead of Juan because it sounds better to my Miami ears. If I told you not to worry about the small stuff—like I'm doing now—I would hope you followed advice, writer fellow. Be proud of yourself."

"How'd you know that I was a writer?"

"You talk in your sleep. I heard you but I'm sorry."

"Don't worry about it."

"We get to feed our faces in a little while. From your looks it might be a good idea for you to eat."

I looked down at my five-eleven stickman body and realized that he had a point. "I eat a lot. I just have this fast metabolism that happens to run in my family. I've been skinny for years and years."

"I meant no harm, friend."

"That's okay, John. Isn't it almost time to eat?" My stomach was up to its old tricks again.

He looked at his watch. "Yeah. It's almost five after six. My jail suit needs to be stained my macaroni. You like the macaroni?"

"I like all of it. Food is probably the only thing that I look forward to in this place."

"Very good attitude. Pleasure from food."

"John, I've been wondering about something."

"And what would that be?"

I smelled his cologne and wished I had something equally as potent to smell on myself which would perhaps elevate my mood and get rid of the nagging "what if" scenarios that repeated themselves like a broken record when I thought about Ellen.

John's business was what? Real estate or perhaps vehicles?

"What kind of business are you in? Real estate or what?"

"Sales, Lester. I'd rather not be specific. You gotta cigarette?"

I pulled a Slam out of my pocket and gave him one.

"Thanks." He put the cigarette in his mouth.

"Need it lit, Johnny?"

"Sure, dude."

I got up from the table, pulled out a cigarette for myself, and walked to the electric cigarette lighter which was on the left wall.

No cigarette lighters of personal origin allowed in jail.

I lit mine after seconds of struggle and walked over to where John was. I handed mine to him and he lit his, handed mine back to me, and coughed.

"Thanks for the light, man. These"—he coughed again—"cigarettes are real strong. Don't try to make me choke."

I sat down and noticed the ashtray.

It looked as if painstaking care had gone into its design and construction. The excellent craftsmanship exhibited in front of me was unusual for something so seemingly functional as an ashtray. I'd have no problems stealing it and taking it home. All I would have to do would be to remember to steal the nice little ashtray.

The fumes from the mop water chemicals seemed to enhance the pleasure of my first drag off of the cigarette.

John hotboxed his cigarette and while doing so he snapped his fingers ten times in quick succession.

There was no music except for the favorite tunes that John might have been able to play at will inside his head.

"It appears as if you're enjoying yourself," I said.

"How very perceptive." He quit hotboxing the cigarette. "You really don't have to stay here, Lester. Miami is a very nice place to stay. Nice weather, plenty of women, everything you want. Think about it."

"Well, maybe. What it is right now is that I've been trying to get over a son of a bitch of a problem."

"Tell me about it, dude. I'll keep it a secret."

I raised my eyebrows. "You really want to know?"

"I think so. It won't hurt me."

"Okay. My girlfriend blew her brains out."

"Oh shit. Did she do it recently?"

"She sure did and I've been trying like hell to deal with it."

"I'm so sorry, man. Is there anything I can do?"

"Be my friend."

"Already taken care of. Come to Florida and I'll get you a job at my place. You can write books while you're there too."

"It might be a good place. The weather down there's supposed to be nice like you said. The place is a writer's paradise. I'll think about it but I still might screw up and have to pay fines."

"If you get in trouble I'll take of everything for you, amigo."

"The food's coming, John. I smell it."

"I'm glad you smell it. How does Miami sound to you?"

"Don't know because I've never been there." I giggled. "Just fine, John. I want to go."

"First things first. Have you forgotten something?"

"Why don't you tell me? Please do."

"It's something you'll probably like. Something called fried chicken. Of course they include cole slaw, mashed potatoes with gravy, and rolls along with the iced tea."

"Far out. I wish they'd bring the T.V. and quit moving like they have hemorrhoids."

"What station tonight, friend? There's supposed to be a World War Two movie coming on channel 47."

"The cable news first and then the movie. Deal?"

"Of course. You want my tea tonight? I'm drinking water because my father had diabetes and went into a diabetic coma. I can tell you a story about him if you wish. Do you?"

"Some other time. I guess you want to watch your sugar."

"Right," John said.

"I'm inclined to be jumpy in my conversations sometimes." I waited to see if what I'd just said would elicit a comment but none came from him. "What about the chicken, John?"

"I don't know. What about it?"

"Do you want all of it?"

He grinned. "I'll bet you'd like it, wouldn't you? As a matter of fact, Lester, I actually do want all of it. Better luck next time. At least you get some extra tea."

"I don't have diabetes," I said.

"Probably not. Any history of hypoglycemia in your family? Do you like sweet things to eat and drink all the time?"

"No on both counts. My father had some liver trouble. In fact he had a lot of liver trouble."

He began playing with his mustache. "So you have liver trouble?"

I shook my head no. "I stayed out in the Sun for too long and developed a little problem."

"Skin cancer can be dangerous. From what I can see it appears that you don't need to stay out in the sunshine for too long, Lester. You're light-skinned and with your dark hair you could probably pass for a vampire."

"Anyway, John, I try to keep in shape. We're an athletic family. Dad played basketball but he never went pro. He told me that he enjoyed being a stock broker more than being a forward."

"And you?"

"I like basketball and jogging. I'm skinny like Dad was as you've already noticed."

"Gain some weight, young guy. You need to keep up your strength in places like this."

Suddenly I heard the rising argument of the two guys who always did argue as if it were a profession.

"Your mother gives blowjobs for free!"

"No she doesn't! She charges a decent five dollars!"

I snickered. "They're at it again, John."

"Tell me about it. There's nothing like friendship."

"I need to gain some weight, huh?"

"Yes. If you go to prison—"

"I know karate."

"They do too, Lester. They're very disturbed and have lots of problems. Gain at least ten pounds, sweet meat."

I let go. "Have you ever been in prison?"

"For a short while, dude. It wasn't fun."

"I'm hungry." As if to respond to what I'd just said I heard the dinner cart coming our way. I looked and noticed that Lloyd had a deluxe T.V. for us tonight instead of a piece of crap.

"Dinnertime, men." He rubbed his fingers and then ran them through his newly-cut silver hair. "I'll bet you two guys are real hungry. If you're not my trip was useless from the start."

"Who's the cocine, old-timer?"

"Alvin Roberts. He's the best cook we've ever had."

"That's good, old-timer. Nice to know," John said.

Lloyd put the television on the floor, hooked up the cable, and plugged it up with aggressive force. He slid the remote to me and I picked it up as it came closer to the dining table.

"That chicken sure smells good. Would it be possible to have it soon as in right now?"

"Coming up." He pushed the trays under the bars along with the iced teas. "There's a good World War Two movie on tonight. My father fought in that war." He paused and then sighed like a man who was uncomfortably aware of his past. "Before I go I'd like to ask both of you if you want any bacalao next week. Do you?"

"I don't like codfish that much. Do you, Lester?"

"Of course I do. I probably won't be here next week but if I am I'll eat it."

"By the way, John, we're having galantine with aspic tomorrow and he'll probably like it," Lloyd said.

"Chicken or veal, Lloyd? Which one?" I asked.

"Veal. You'll be ready, won't—"

"You bet. John might not like the real meals, though."

"Speak for yourself, friend. Both have an excellent taste but why feed us so well?"

"Because Lester's a famous author. Eat good, gentlemen. If you want some more cole slaw just holler." He smiled and as he walked away he began to whistle.

"Lester? Aren't you going to get the food?"

I looked down at the trays and teas just below the bars.

I had the feeling something wasn't exactly right but I wasn't sure what it was.

I looked at John and his entire body seemed impossibly narrow while the sounds of his movements and breath were amplified and at the same time distorted so that he sounded demonic. I closed my eyes and opened them and he was back to normal.

"I'm okay, John. I think I need to get more sleep."

"Get the food first."

I got up and walked to the bars. I picked up both trays and set them on the table and then I got the teas, appreciating the fact that I'd get some extra liquid refreshment.

The cigarettes made my mouth dry.

"Dinner is served," I said.

"You can have the chicken. I'll turn on the tube in a little while unless you mind."

"Why should I mind?"

"You shouldn't, scribe. I'll bet T.V. gives you ideas."

"Sometimes. Let's eat."

He handed me his tea and then we both ate like dogs that'd been starved. In one minute only the bones were left on my chicken pieces so I wolfed down the cole slaw and mashed potatoes.

"When you finish your extra tea get me some water from the sink. Does that agree with you?" John asked.

"Sure."

"Great, man. De nada."

"They don't always treat people in jail this good," I said.

"Absolutely not. It helps me a great deal that you're a writer and that a lot of those cops like to buy your books," John said.

"What's the word for writer in Spanish?"

"Escritor. Why did you want to know?"

"Just curious."

He sniffed and then folded his arms. "As soon as I get out of here I'm going back to Florida. I assume you want to go down there too. Correct or incorrect, Lester?"

"Correct. Ellen blew her brains out and I really don't have any reason to stay in Alabama. Staying here'll most likely bring back pain in my brain that I can't live with."

"Yes, yes. Come to Florida and have some fun. I'm going to turn on the news."

"What do you think—"

"Let's watch the news, Lester." He turned on the T.V. and, unfortunately, there was no sound emanating from it.

"Great." The screen showed file footage of the Cuban Missile Crisis along with pictures of Kennedy and Kruschev. On the bottom of the screen was a news bulletin which said: President Shepard gives Cuban government two weeks to kick out foreign advisers and remove missiles or suffer consequences***Cuban leaders deny any missiles with atomic warheads are in their country and tell Washington to prove it.

"I guess you don't want to come to Miami," John said.

"Correct."

"I'll turn off the television. We'll both feel better."

"Excellent choice," I said.

He turned it off.

I finished the last bites of my supper and got into bed. I made sure the pillow was right and then I relaxed and listened to men in other cells argue about chicken and poker money.

The salesman hadn't been kidding about the computer. This coming Wednesday I'd be released from jail and if I played my cards right there'd be no need to worry. I'd started a crisis because I really couldn't believe what the man told me about my new gizmo and soon it would be time to undo the damage. When I blinked first this time like the Russians did I would have no loss but my gain would come in the form of beautiful, wonderful Ellen.

Time passed quickly and a guy I met named David told me a story.

His father had been a bomber pilot in the early sixties. If World War Three had started due to the hostile environment created by the presence of missiles in Cuba David's father was one of the men who would have taken a bomber to good old Moscow. I wasn't going to let my action with my weird computer be the one to start some shit. Years of taking life for granted were comfortable years for me but they had to end thanks to a reality that should've been impossible.

What was really good was that John had given me his card which had his phone number on it. I'd work for him in a heartbeat even if I were in the middle of writing a masterpiece of a novel.

Suddenly my incarceration was over. I was happy.

I was walking to the lobby to call a cab.

The same clothes that I had on when the scarecrow of a cop had arrested me were the same ones I had on now.

From rags to riches and riches to rags. Wow! Golly!

Had I caused Ellen to whoops her brains onto the floor of her nice apartment? Whether I did or not was not even worth considering. The alien computer with its unique output device was going to bring back ladylove and I'd be the first one to greet her. The urn that rested on her father's library desk would be empty soon enough and my tortured and overworked mind would and could relax.

I sat down in front of a pay phone which happened to be the only one in the lobby. As I looked men walked through the economical, spare lobby with smiles that probably came from taking a good shit. One of them pointed at me and mimed smoking a cigarette with eyebrows raised.

I reached into my right pants pocket and pulled out a quarter. I made the call to the cab company as short and sweet as possible because the smiling guys were arguing about packs of cigarettes.

"Hurry up, please." My heart beat faster. I looked at my long fingernails with crap underneath them. I looked out the lobby window and saw my ride.

If the missiles hit, which of course they would if launched, then the thermonuclear explosions might have unexpected effects on the computer. The possible effect and or effects gave me another reason to be urgent. One possible reason not be urgent about deleting the offending statements in my file was that my mouth tasted like shit and if I didn't tell the driver to stop I'd miss an opportunity to quench my almost insane thirst. Pleasure should come before business.

I walked out to the cab, got in, and issued instructions to the driver. As we left my temporary home it began to rain.

I was free, white, and thirty-one.

Getting my freedom back meant keeping traditions so, to celebrate my good fortune, I groped for my Slams and went through the process before taking a puff of the cigarette that always worked wonders. The cab whizzed by places I knew like the back of my hand. I whooshed and the driver replied by turning on the heat in the cramped cab.

I looked at the landmarks.

Saving the world when you're the one who did something to almost cause it to end was funny. The stupidity of life never ceased to amaze me.

I looked at the driver's I.D. on the dashboard and noticed that he was in the military.

"Kind of rainy, huh?" I asked.

He sniffed and didn't say a word.

He was all smooth efficiency and get the job done. There seemed to be no room for mistakes in my cabdriver's personality but there was no need to criticize him for that.

I saw my house. "Stop up there."

"When you get out don't get too wet. These October rains can kill you." He glanced at me and grinned. "How long did you stay in the hotel back there?"

"The jail, right?"

"Yeah."

"A few weeks." The car stopped in front of my house and I got my money ready. "How much?"

"Twelve-fifty. I'd prefer cash."

"You got it." I handed him the money. "It was fun riding shotgun with you."

He waved the cash with his thick, almost meatloaf-sized hands before giving me the change. "Don't spend it all in one place."

"I won't." I got out and pulled my doorkey out of my pants pocket in a panicked way.

Just a few problems left. Excellent.

As I walked up the steps to the house my thoughts turned to the little details that I sometimes neglected to think about. I unlocked the front door and walked into the den.

I was glad that they'd put my car back in the driveway. Real glad but not sad.

I glanced at the digital clock on the wall which with red numerals said 3:58.

The missiles weren't supposed to be launched until 4:30 so I decided to go to the kitchen in order to feed my face and end the dryness of my mouth.

I fixed the food and then pulled a cold can of Throat's Root Beer out of the refrigerator before sitting down at the table. I opened the can and practically inhaled the contents. I took a bite of the sandwich and the power went off immediately.

I didn't need to worry either way. The entire city was a target and I'd be one of the very first to die when and if the missile hit. If by luck the power came back on I'd go on with the plan.

Minutes passed and no AC came through the wires to rescue me.

I looked through the kitchen window at the rainshower while my heart beat furiously in my chest. As I worried and found creative ways to pray thunder unintentionally punctuated my thoughts.

I remembered when I turned eight and my mother cut my birthday cake while my brother watched Radiation Man.

I'd had a very good brother, not a bad one. He'd gone on to become a prosperous real estate agent while I struggled with freelance assignments. Life had been mostly unremarkable and boring and yet this really couldn't be the time to kiss my ass goodbye.

I cracked my knuckles and the power came back on. I got up violently and ran to the bedroom computer as fast as possible.

I had seven minutes.

I turned it on, double-clicked the word processor icon, and waited a few seconds. I moved the mouse until the arrow was on Files and then clicked. I opened the file which had the offending words and deleted them without hesitation. As I looked the computer began typing a message which said: Hey, Lester! John the computer here. It was nice of you to save the world. Go to Miami with Ellen, man. You'll love it! I guarantee you work down there if you want it, friend.

So Mr. Garcia was the computer. The strange way he'd looked in jail could've been his bad side trying to take over. The thing to do about the unusual power of my new toy was to use it again and again.

"Ellen Rainwoode, you're coming back tomorrow." I typed: Ellen Rainwoode is coming back to life tomorrow and her first destination is going to be my house.

I stretched and felt my bones adjusting themselves and then yawned before concentrating again.

I saved the bit about Ellen and then typed: I have twenty cartons of Slams in my closet.

Actually I just had two packs left but it was worth checking out.

I got up, walked to my closet, and opened the door. I looked and saw the twenty cartons neatly stacked on the upper shelf of my closet in groups of four.

"Son-of-a-bitch!!"

This was good.

I walked over to the computer and, with every intention of using it again, shut if off.

I walked to the bathroom and took a quick shower. After putting on some cologne and putting on my robe I walked back to the bedroom. As I entered the bedroom I noticed a new problem.

Just because the water had leaked from the ceiling onto the computer didn't mean it was the end of the world.

I walked to the den, picked up the remote, and turned the tube on. As I scanned the news channels there was no mention at all about any missile crisis.

I could probably fix the computer after taking a course in computer repair but the really important factor was Ellen. With her the world of computers and electronics was very, very insignificant.

I went to the kitchen to get a bag of chips.

Tomorrow was a new day.

ABOUT THE AUTHOR

Mr. Carlton Gordy's previously published poem—"One Man's Decision"—was recently included in a collection of poetry. He graduated from Long Ridge Writer's Group and completed the Writer's Digest Novel Writing Workshop course. He's had some short stories published in newsletters but remembers an essay he wrote in the sixth grade regarding how great his country was and why. Since it was required as part of his English course he says that he got "hooked" on writing from that moment on.